299

Sleepin

to Marylile,
a great person
to work with!

Jennifer

Also by Jennifer Mitton

Fadimatu

Sleeping with the Insane

JENNIFER MITTON

GOOSE LANE

Published with the assistance of the Canada Council, 1995.

These stories have been published in the following journals and anthologies: "The Last Ferry" in *Left Bank;* "Not a Day Goes By" in *LiNQ;* "Phantom Pain" in *The Malahat Review*; "Rules of the Living" in *Tickle Ace*; "Sleeping with the Insane" in *The Fiddlehead*; "Spies" in *The New Quarterly* and *Best Canadian Stories*; "Untying Elinor" in *Prairie Journal of Canadian Literature;* "The Weepers" in *The Malahat Review* and *Words We Call Home*.

The author wishes to thank the Canada Council for its generous support for the completion of the manuscript.

Cover photograph from the *Fragmentos* series (1994) by Magda Mujica. Hand-coloured silver gelatin print on paper. Reproduced with permission of the artist.

Book design by Julie Scriver.

Printed and bound in Canada by Imprimerie Gagné.

10 9 8 7 6 5 4 3 2

Canadian Cataloguing in Publication Data

Mitton, Jennifer, 1955-
Sleeping with the insane
ISBN 0-86492-157-8

I. Title.

PS8576.I8875S53 1995 C813'.54 C95-950056-1
PR9199.3.M58S53 1995

Goose Lane Editions
469 King Street
Fredericton, New Brunswick
CANADA E3B 1E5

CONTENTS

A PERIOD OF WEAKNESS

As she cycled up to the studio on the first day of her drawing class, Jocelyn wasn't fantasizing about sleeping with a man twenty years her senior. She would have been unable to imagine it. She was thinking about what could happen during the two-week course. She might — although it was unlikely — get a reference for the École des Beaux-Arts. She might even find a lover.

The instructor, Monsieur Hamid, was a small, dark man whose chief source of power was his intense preoccupation with something abstract, or, at least, invisible. Jocelyn could not take her eyes off him. The fact that there were no male students must have added to his charisma and prompted an unexpected fantasy. But Jocelyn could not, even in her mind, go past the obvious obstacle: Monsieur Hamid was an old man.

At twenty-six Jocelyn had made love only once. This had occurred on a camping trip when she was still a teenager, and her lover had been a youth himself — she remembered him telling her he was a pre-medical student. But that was about all — what she remembered of that night had little to do with him. She remembered the way the evening light fell on the cool sand as she carried water down through the cedars from the campground tap, and most of all she remembered waking up during the night, holding in place a part of the vast, living sand with her four frozen limbs. Then, curling into the boy's warmth, she watched her memories and creations appear and fade in a long, patient slide show.

Eventually she felt the eyeache of tiredness, and lost interest in her thoughts, and lay listening to the boy's heavy breath as she waited for sleep. Always, one of her arms or legs was cramped, and she wanted to fling herself into a new position. But there wasn't room, and she didn't want to wake the boy: there was virtue in accepting her discomfort. She hadn't been acquainted with insomnia long enough to resent it. If anything she suspected it was useful, helping her to remain supremely alert should this be a great adventure.

Now she was more mature. She had made hundreds of difficult crossings from her mind's daily activity to the field of sleep, and she had discovered that few of them ever heralded true adventure.

At university she had become acquainted with cynicism. Each time she had passed the notice board she saw the spray-painted proclamation, *The Heart Pumps Blood*. Sometimes she felt a hardening of her resolve to shun fantasy: the strange, curly-haired boy who sat doodling through each French class was probably a self-centred bore. At other times she felt a quickening of the very urges she was trying to avoid: she imagined the quiet boy following her from class one day, showing her the sketch of her he had drawn from memory the night before; he hadn't been able to stop thinking about her, he couldn't sleep, he was failing his courses . . .

Then, just as he was reaching out to touch her face, his hand warm, steady, sensitive . . . there it was again on the notice board: *The Heart Pumps Blood*. Logic and emotion, heart and head. By the time Jocelyn graduated she knew that there was no division. There was no such thing as a life adventure, there was only adrenaline; there was no mind, but only a particular combination of electrical synapses; and there was probably no such thing as love, but only instinctual need in all its forms and pleasing fulfilments. And needs, it turned out, were hardly ever fundamental. Most needs, desires, weaknesses and compulsions — call them what you will — could be extinguished with the correct conditions.

But now she was in France, her birthplace and, perhaps, her true home. In France the heart could still do more than pump blood. Here there were layers of experience to be examined, and there were professionals who welcomed the task. Psychiatrists here were still esteemed, they listened with compassion, they took notes and analysed. They took the mind seriously.

These thoughts were in Jocelyn's mind as she locked her bicycle and carried her portfolio up the steps to the studio, and it occurred to her that while she was in France, she might allow herself a certain respect for her fantasies. So she did nothing, on that first day of class, to resist the notion that Monsieur Hamid was to figure in a new adventure. She had been unable to sleep until she heard the first birds and came to class with a perspiring, self-conscious energy. She told herself that Monsieur Hamid must be used to young women staring at him, brooding over their confused memories of first lovers and dampness and chills.

What she remembered most clearly about the first class was the care Monsieur Hamid took in arranging his strange still life of undergarments. Standing at the model's bench, he fashioned a dark velvet blanket into hills and valleys, then landscaped them with lacy undergarments he took from a packsack.

Throughout his opening lecture he interrupted himself to fuss with the arrangement. He poked straps and bits of elasticized lace this way and that with his small brown hands, sucking in air through his teeth, grunting, stepping back to appraise his work. He was obsessed.

Well! He was old. Perhaps he had spent his time preening and strutting as a youth; perhaps now he preferred to enter his fantasies by an easier route.

Jocelyn wanted it to be clear that if she had hard feelings after her failed seductions, she blamed herself.

The class began. As tired as she was, Jocelyn felt excited by the ridiculous scene. Later that night she would describe the small, severe Monsieur Hamid in a letter to a friend, instantly, though unintentionally, making him seem larger than life. She fell asleep in a fever. Although she was born in Normandy, Jocelyn had grown up in the west island town of Pointe Claire, Quebec, and, as was fitting, had the pale skin and equivocal restraint typical of both regions: she was as liable to be stirred by her own words written after midnight as she was by an actual event occurring at midday.

Letters were one thing, but she wished there had been a girlfriend to watch it all with. Someone from one of her university classes. A friend who liked to laugh.

But the next easel had been empty. And after class? She couldn't even gossip with her roommate Jérôme. He was on a three-week course in Strasbourg learning how to plant telephone wires deep underground. She and Jérôme had met through a laundromat notice board and found a charming flat on a walkway inaccessible to cars, two hundred steps above the street. They had become friends. Still, there was always the uneasiness that came with having to guard sexual boundaries: Jérôme was bisexual, and Jocelyn wanted a wholehearted lover for her second experience.

In his introductory lecture Monsieur Hamid talked about the École des Beaux-Arts. They must work hard if they wanted a recommendation, he was saying. They would need top marks. Even then he couldn't promise anything. He refused to compromise. And it was clear from their portfolios, he remarked with bitterness, that no one had put serious effort into their art.

His charisma must have been stunning; the young women sat

listening in frozen silence, their mouths limp. It may be that there was something so acutely sexual about Monsieur Hamid's tirade that the words didn't matter.

When he finished there was a pause, and then a woman with a well-groomed voice asked about the model. She gestured firmly at the undergarments arranged on the velvet. Was the model late?

"Not at all," was all Monsieur Hamid said. "As you can see, Mademoiselle, there is no live model." He chose not to explain the still life of women's underclothing. The students were to set up their easels and sketch the still life using any medium they wished. Everything was at once clear and absurd.

When the scraping and dragging and accidents with easels were done with, a latecomer pushed open the door. It was a girl so beautiful that at least a few of the students made helpless gasping sounds.

Evidently Monsieur Hamid knew her. "Nathalia!" he exclaimed, and rushed to help her hang up her jacket. She allowed him to hold her arm while she gazed out the open window, her eyelids heavy, her perfume drifting lightly into the room. He held her as if he feared she might fly away, and whispered to her the essentials of the assignment. He dropped her arm to rummage in the corner for an easel. Having found one that was unbroken, he dragged it to the best available space, thereby blocking another student's view. "I'm sorry," he told that student, and then rushed back to Nathalia at the window, coaxing her to begin. Wouldn't she like to lay out her drawing materials?

It became clear that the beautiful girl had no drawing materials. Jocelyn watched while Monsieur Hamid scurried to take up a collection — a sheet of Canson, a stick of charcoal, a bit of kneaded eraser — anything they could spare, he whispered.

Jocelyn's desire to capture Monsieur Hamid's attention grew, inflated by her envy of the beautiful Nathalia. Half of his attention would do. One quarter. She wanted to spit on her first sketch because she sensed that the composition would not attract his interest. She watched Nathalia settle into a trance of carefree and unmistakeably clumsy sketching. To think that she herself had cycled up that never-ending hill through the inferno of noise and scowling workmen, her portfolio banging, the strings unknotting themselves against her knees, found her way through the maze of the eleventh arrondissement to this evil-smelling studio, arrived in time to repair a broken-down easel with fishing line so it would tolerate the weight of her battered portfolio, listened to the instructor's depressing lecture about the almost certain impossibility of entering the École des Beaux-Arts, and had now donated one of her three best sheets of Canson to the beautiful Nathalia. To think.

At the short break a sallow, fleshy girl approached Jocelyn to confide that she knew Nathalia. As the lead singer in a local rock band she had been to parties with Nathalia and Nathalia's guitarist boyfriend. ("*You're* a lead singer?" Jocelyn had to ask.)

Yes, the girl said. And Nathalia's boyfriend was on the road a lot. A *lot*, if Jocelyn knew what she meant. Nathalia lived with him at the top of an incredibly beautiful hill inaccessible to cars. Probably Cézanne had painted that hill. Anyway, to reach the house you had to climb five hundred steps from the street. No wonder Nathalia's fit, the girl remarked. But she was certain that Nathalia's guitarist boyfriend was not always on the road touring when he was away from Nathalia. How many times had she seen him sitting in the next town drinking beer?

Jocelyn shrugged. Suddenly, the charming apartment she shared with Jérôme two hundred steps above the street was less than noteworthy. *Nathalia* had a guitarist boyfriend! *Nathalia* lived with her boyfriend five hundred steps above the street! (And that night Jocelyn looked up Nathalia in her name dictionary. *Nathalia: breath of life*. So, the beautiful Nathalia had what she needed to walk up those five hundred steps.)

Monsieur Hamid called for the students to resume their drawing. He continued to pace and to make imperceptible adjustments to the undergarment arrangement for nearly an hour, and then he announced a long break and, with a flourish, pulled all the undergarments from the model's bench.

Jocelyn stood by the sink scratching with her nails through the soapy charcoal on her fingers. She moved ahead when it was her turn and eventually rinsed them under the cold faucet.

For the thousandth time she remembered her first and only lover.

But it was useless to try to seduce Monsieur Hamid. She shook her hands dry and left the glum studio to buy a piece of fruit from the grocer across the street. Was it bird droppings the studio smelled of? Or gouache?

When she returned from the grocer's with a pear, there was a mobylette chained to a parking meter in front of the studio and a dark-haired youth at the door. He sat leaning against the railing, one leg outstretched into the sun along the top landing and the other foot set carelessly on a lower step. Jocelyn stared at him: even from across the street his was beauty to take one's breath away.

The street was deserted, the air chalky and slow-moving. Jocelyn strolled as slowly as she could, the better to observe the young man. She alternated bites from the pear and the chocolate bar she had brought from home until she reached the studio. She could no longer look directly at the handsome youth. She drew in her breath, certain that something magical was about to happen, perhaps when she reached the top of the steps and had to cross over his legs.

Jocelyn's foot was on the first step when Nathalia ran out, plucked the cigarette from the boy's fingers and kissed him on the mouth. She crouched beside him, smoking, while Jocelyn slowly climbed the stairs — if the youth hadn't been there she would have taken the stairs two at a time. Her self-consciousness made her feel like a heat-stricken animal. Nothing happened. She stepped over the youth's outstretched leg and into the gloom of the foyer. When she glanced around from the inner courtyard she saw the youth stand and pull Nathalia up with him. She turned before she had to see them kiss.

Back in the studio she felt hot and out of breath. She saw that most of the students' sketches had little to do with the facts of life, not even the life of undergarments. Nathalia's drawings were notably uninteresting and wooden, and yet she had signed each one. And why shouldn't she? Nathalia had the luck to be beautiful, and for this she had become accustomed to all sorts of misdirected praise and developed an overly high opinion of her own talents.

Monsieur Hamid was finishing his new still life arrangement. A different assortment of brassieres, camisoles and panties fell in new patterns over the dark velvet.

The other students drifted back in, smelling of chocolate and lipstick and cigarettes. Monsieur Hamid waited at Nathalia's easel, and leaned close, whispering cautions as she traced over the initial and already graceless contour lines of a new sketch.

But why wouldn't he lean close to such a girl? Even her name was lucky. If you could give your daughter such a beautiful name, *Nathalia: breath of life*, why would you choose *Jocelyn*?

Monsieur Hamid's critiques of all the other students were harsh, and on that first day one girl stumbled out to the courtyard in tears. The sallow lead singer clumped after her and the two of them stayed in the courtyard by the door, the smell of their cigarette smoke trailing in underneath.

Monsieur Hamid was wise to conclude ten minutes early.

"So then. We meet at the same time tomorrow." He stood behind Nathalia as she packed up her materials, and Jocelyn heard him say under his breath, "I hope that my son will not keep you from your drawing assignment tonight." Even though his tone was more teasing than harsh, Nathalia didn't smile.

"Thierry won't keep me from anything," she said.

As if it weren't astonishing enough that the handsome youth could be Hamid's son, Thierry chose that moment to open the studio door.

He stood talking with his father, ignoring Nathalia as she packed up her portfolio and borrowed materials. Then he turned, and at his signal Nathalia trailed across the courtyard and down the steps after him to his mobylette.

Jocelyn had the misfortune to follow them both.

Unlocking her own bicycle, she watched Thierry strap Nathalia's portfolio to the back of his mobylette. He mounted. Nathalia squeezed up close, leaving a length of leatherette space behind her.

Jocelyn gazed after them, comparing the son with his father. As a younger man, Monsieur Hamid must in addition to his own powerful charisma have had his son's looks. Although Thierry, she sensed, was bolder, less constrained in sexual matters than his father could ever have been.

Of course none of this was the point. Thierry was Nathalia's boyfriend, and Monsieur Hamid was too old. Jocelyn needed a portfolio. She needed a high recommendation from Monsieur Hamid. She needed some sleep. *The Heart Pumps Blood*. It was crazy to indulge a weakness for what was not your concern.

She was pouring coffee the next morning when she saw a movement outside. She opened the kitchen door, preparing to shout *Nom de dieu!* at one of the dull, defecating dogs, and to throw something to chase it off the walkway.

But it was Monsieur Hamid's son Thierry — the boy who carried Nathalia on his mobylette when her guitarist boyfriend was out of town. Obviously he was without his mobylette; he would have had to lock it on the street below, unless he wanted to haul it up the steps to the walkway.

How long had he been there? And what could he be doing? She had a sudden, wild certainty that he had, after all, taken special notice of her the day before at the drawing studio — perhaps he had been enchanted with her profile as she stepped over his outstretched leg — and that he had climbed the two hundred steps to her apartment to see her. "Nathalia is beautiful, yes. That is undeniable," he would say. "But *so* dull. . . . While *you* . . . "

She unlatched the kitchen doors. "Do you need something?" In her own confusion she followed his gaze to the sun-washed block of apartments across the ravine. Her voice was affected by the ugliness of her greyed nightgown and socks, which she should have taken off and exchanged for something summery with her first cup of coffee.

"Nothing at all." Thierry laughed, seeing her distress. He ground out his cigarette and saluted her as he opened the gate to the neighbouring garden. What could he want next door at the psychiatrist's? Could he be a patient?

Jocelyn felt her mind empty.

She showered and brought in the laundry she had hung the day before, folding each piece as she unclipped it from the string. Her one nice set of underwear — a brassiere and panties with lace and a floral pattern — the one she had planned to use for Monsieur Hamid's still life homework assignment — was missing.

"Light-coloured lingerie, draped over a dark surface," Monsieur Hamid had said. "Something simple. A simple arrangement."

Simple! Was she going to drop three hundred francs to buy the kind of undergarments he had arranged for them at the studio? So that she could complete one homework assignment? She wanted to weep. She remembered hanging them on the line the night before, just as the sun was setting. There, beside the sad family of cotton briefs and light-support brassieres, all grey after an unfortunate cycle with one of Jérôme's black bodyshirts.

She leaned over the crumbling stone wall separating the walkway from the ravine. A scrap of paper from the bakery was caught in the brambles. She watched it struggling and thought of the youth who had gone next door to Dr. Ilse's.

From the neighbours on the other side — the young couple who quarrelled — came a smell of sauerkraut and sausage; from the psychiatrist's side, a scent of flowers. Dr. Ilse and her little girl, Lucie, occupied the entire block of apartments at the dead end of the *traverse*. Jocelyn had never seen a man who might be Lucie's father come to visit, although for a time she inspected each male patient, and she had concluded that inspections and calculations were useless in the area of love.

Now she brought her easel into the kitchen and set it up so she could keep watch on the clothesline, and — why not — on Dr. Ilse's gate.

Even the dogs were quiet on this summer morning. She hung her second-best brassiere over one of Jérôme's dark T-shirts and arranged them over a kitchen chair. As she drew she felt obliged to invent a bit of lace.

Thierry latched the gate to Dr. Ilse's garden behind him just before noon. He ducked under the empty clothesline to light a cigarette. As she observed him Jocelyn concluded he was without question her type. She used quiet movements to unclip her homework sketch without attracting his attention, and began to draw his profile. She imagined the fragrance of his dark hair and the moisture along the backs of his hands.

A cigarette, she had read, lasts about seven minutes — enough time to get a likeness. The instant Thierry left she found Dr. Ilse's number in the directory and called her. She knew Dr. Ilse received patients at home, but Thierry had gone in at 11:45 and come out at 11:58. Surely Dr. Ilse did not conduct ten-minute sessions?

It would have to remain a mystery, because no one answered the telephone.

The next day Monsieur Hamid was late for class.

The air was unbearably hot and, cycling up to the *atelier*, Jocelyn imagined herself to be the only one in the city not lying, arms and legs spread wide, under an effective ceiling fan. She was not surprised to find the studio courtyard empty, the floor still sleeping under sand and tracks from the day before. Who would come on a day this hot? Jocelyn sat for a moment. She needed to cool off before the ride home, even if it was mostly downhill.

She was still there when another drawing student drifted in and sat on the bench opposite. The girl looked dull and unwilling and after a moment leaned her head against the wall and closed her eyes. Other students joined them, and when they were half a dozen, Jocelyn opened her sketchbook, thinking she might construct an interesting composition. But as soon as she had the book open on her knees the idea vanished. She waited, but nothing came to replace it. She felt her knees begin to sweat under the plastic-coated book, and she returned it to her cardboard portfolio. Exhausted by this gesture, she closed her own eyes. Several times she drifted in and out of sleep. Monsieur Hamid was over an hour late.

He apologized for the unavoidable delay and suggested they begin immediately using the new still life. He unlocked the door, and they all shuffled in.

Jocelyn took a moment to rinse her face and drink from the tap at the clean-up sink. She was putting on orange lipstick without a mirror when she heard Nathalia and Thierry come in. "If you want . . . it's all the same to me," Nathalia was saying. Thierry seemed not to have heard. He put down her portfolio and bag and turned to leave. Nathalia jumped in front of him and held her face up to be kissed. Jocelyn noticed Nathalia was also wearing orange lipstick. It concentrated your attention on her mouth. Jocelyn wanted to take this as a sign . . . a sign that she too could at least be noticed? But perhaps she should not have put on quite so much. She patted her lips into the palm of her hand and stared a moment at the perfect print before she rubbed it into her jeans.

There were some months when Jocelyn daydreamed of sex. This cycle, she was certain to be preoccupied with fantasies of Monsieur Hamid and his son Thierry. The problem was, Monsieur Hamid seemed the sort of man who felt superior to physical acts. At the moment Monsieur Hamid was staring out over the rust-coloured roof. What could anybody know about his body underneath those robes? He dressed like a monk. For the first time she intuited sinews and mustiness; the thought was unsavoury and killed her sexual desire.

The other students had begun to plot their compositions. The new still life was a modernist jumble of plain slips and functional brassieres against a neutral grey drapery, and yet it had a confusing sexual aura. Jocelyn felt safe in assuming this rich sexuality was a product of her own fantasy and projection until she heard Monsieur Hamid gasp, and, turning, she saw that one student's drawing was far from being an accurate representation of functional underclothes. It was a crude but deeply suggestive sketch of the beautiful Nathalia. This too was confusing until you looked at Nathalia, who was not drawing at all. Then you realized that the still life was composed — most probably entirely — of Nathalia's own undergarments. It was natural that the more sensitive students felt compelled to study Nathalia and to incorporate her plush torso and her creamy arms as the ground — the support, as it were — for the underclothing.

Monsieur Hamid said nothing, but resumed his slow walk outside the circle of easels.

It was as if a fresh breeze had passed through the room; one by one, the other students began new sketches, this time focussing directly on Nathalia. Jocelyn could see the class exhibit already: *Beautiful girl with her underclothes.* Still, she could not help but feel inspired, and she sensed the air around her energized as the students, most of them for the first time, tried to transfer what they saw in the three dimensions of the crowded studio onto the vast flatness of their paper.

The instant Jocelyn had captured the gesture of Nathalia's head and torso she was impatient for Monsieur Hamid to see her sketch. But he walked slowly, slowly; he wasn't halfway around to her. She began to hate him.

Now he was standing behind Nathalia. Pointing to something in the sketch she had abandoned, he put his other hand on her shoulder.

In spite of her intelligence, Jocelyn could not understand that Hamid was not a middle-aged man caught by diminishing hope and desire. He was touching the girl, yes, but with the kind of firmness you use with a dog you wish to train. "Look how you've rendered the cup of this brassiere. It looks like plaster," he said. Nathalia shrugged, and Hamid coughed and began to walk again.

Jocelyn had planned to leave early to go to the health clinic. Her insomnia had shown no improvement since the end of spring term — if anything, it was worse now with the start of the summer studio class. She had been reluctant to see a doctor, imagining his — or her — professional smirk after she revealed the running number of years she had been celibate. Perhaps it was thanks to Thierry that she could now imagine asking for a referral to see a psychiatrist. After all, Thierry, handsome as he was, was seeing a psychiatrist. She would point out to the doctor that she happened to live next door to a psychiatrist . . . not to say that it was absolutely necessary that she be referred to Dr. Ilse, but in terms of convenience . . .

The other students were still so intent on their studies of Nathalia that Jocelyn could have made any amount of noise packing up her materials and leaving the studio. From the top of the steps she saw Thierry locking his mobylette.

"Class doesn't finish for another hour," she called. Being out of the running gave her a certain confidence.

"I know." He gazed down the street, and for the second time she marvelled at his resemblance to Monsieur Hamid.

She got on her bicycle but, following a sudden impulse, turned at the corner by the grocer's. Pulling her bicycle to the wall, she could see Thierry through the grocer's window.

Something compelled her to wait there, watching Thierry even though he was doing nothing out of the ordinary. He took a book from his bag and sat reading. A quarter of an hour passed, and Nathalia appeared in the studio doorway. Thierry called at her to hurry up and she gave an ambiguous little wave, and descended the steps with exaggerated slowness. She allowed him to strap her gear to the mobylette and then she climbed on and shrugged against him as if she were caught in an advertisement daydream, and only then did Jocelyn realize it would now be too late to reach the clinic.

She also noticed that the red-cheeked grocer was tossing her suspicious glances as he tended his bins of vegetables. She chose a pear and brought it in to his scale. He articulated the price in old francs, and together they watched Thierry sail off with his prize, tossing, tossing down the street between the parked cars.

Jocelyn strapped her own portfolio to her bicycle handlebars. She was now in the sort of mood in which she always got a puncture, and she waited for it as one would for a friend, braking continually down the long hill.

Her tires were, nevertheless, both hard when she reached her *traverse*. She lugged her bicycle up the stairs to the walkway into a thick sunset. The facing block of apartments was flooded in pinks and golds. In the box she shared with Jérôme, there was a letter from her Italian travelling friend, Césare. She had not been forgotten.

She whirled dry a salad and ate it with the remainder of the morning baguette. Césare's letter contained nothing more than a five-line postcard from Norway. There on vacation, he had run into relatives of her neighbour, Dr. Ilse, whom he had liked very much. He hoped Jocelyn would send his regards.

That he liked Dr. Ilse was not what bothered Jocelyn. And she wasn't looking for a romance with Césare. She had almost never wished he were her boyfriend. It was just that she felt sure he had sent dozens, even hundreds of these postcards. He always did. She could have slept with him on her birthday — her twentieth, it had been — if she hadn't stood up, rearranged her clothes, and whispered something about going back to the dance. Césare was friendly about her refusal, as he might have been about thousands of refusals. Should she have slept with him? It would have brought the count of her lovers up to two, and shortened her period of celibacy to what she thought might be a more normal number of years.

She walked to the park overlooking the sea. The sun had set, and already the slats of the painted iron bench were too cold to endure more than a few minutes. She started back again through the damp grass, feeling her entire life was a failure.

At the café on the corner a figure inside caught her attention: it was Dr. Ilse, waving and smiling. She wanted Jocelyn to join her at her window table. Dr. Ilse put her detective novel on a thick file — notes for a patient, Jocelyn guessed — and offered Jocelyn wine from her carafe. She laughed when Jocelyn said she preferred steamed milk. "I want all French to behave the way they did in my schoolbooks," said Dr. Ilse. Her teasing made Jocelyn happy, and her assumption that Jocelyn was French gave her added courage to ask the psychiatrist questions. Why had Dr. Ilse come to France, and did she like life in the Midi? Did she prefer it to life in Paris? What about her life outside of work?

How did she like living with her small daughter Lucie on a *traverse* no cars could reach? Were these questions too personal?

Not at all, said Dr. Ilse. She liked Marseille, although in the beginning she had found the daily rhythm strange and had no doubt antagonized a few patients by insisting on a schedule more suited to a northern climate. And her reason for becoming a psychiatrist, she said, was that after a long period of weakness for men, she had entered an even worse time of weakness for all troubled souls. Disastrous times, both of them, she laughed. But look at Lucie. When she first met Hamid, he already had a fifteen-year-old son. Perhaps Jocelyn had seen Thierry at the drawing studio, waiting for his father?

The story had so many chapters . . . but look at Lucie, Dr. Ilse said again. Lucie, the child she had conceived with Hamid in the period of their new love: wasn't Lucie the perfect gift to come from a *désastre*, from the stars?

Jocelyn nodded. Of course. Lucie. From the stars. But *Monsieur Hamid*? Dr. Ilse's lover? And Thierry, her stepson?

"I have seen Thierry at the studio," Jocelyn said. "But I don't think he was waiting for Monsieur Hamid. He comes to pick up a student, a very beautiful girl. Nathalia."

Dr. Ilse raised her eyebrows, but only for a moment. She went on. "Before Lucie was born we made a decision to live apart," she said. "Since then I've blamed myself. I have terrible weaknesses . . . "

"It's better than having no weakness at all," Jocelyn said, wanting suddenly to change the subject of conversation. "By the way — I got a letter from Césare, you know, my Italian student friend, the one who visited in the spring. We nearly had a fling years ago. Anyway, he was terribly impressed by you. He gives his fond regards."

Dr. Ilse's eyebrows were still raised. "Césare," she said, trying to give the name the meaning of memory.

Jocelyn nodded. "Césare." But it didn't matter. There was

nothing more to say. She saw Dr. Ilse shiver and suggested they walk back to the *traverse*.

That night Jocelyn dreamed of the youth Thierry in an angry, growling confrontation with his father. From a different direction came banging sounds and a child's frightened cries. It came to her that Thierry and Hamid were in her dream, while the banging and crying belonged to a different part of reality — the waking part. Someone *was* banging at her kitchen door, and a child was crying.

Dr. Ilse stood on the walkway shivering with Lucie. As soon as Jocelyn opened the door Lucie stopped crying. "Dog," she said, pointing to the back courtyard with intelligent authority. The dogs settled down to peace-making growls.

"Loads of silly dogs," Jocelyn said. "Dr. Ilse. What happened?"

Dr. Ilse's voice was high with fright. "It's Hamid! He's tearing my office apart . . . my files. . . . Can you come? I'm sorry," she muttered. "It's the middle of the night."

"It doesn't matter. . . . Of course I'll come." Jocelyn took Lucie's hand and urged the psychiatrist not to worry. Still, she couldn't imagine how she would be able to help. Perhaps Dr. Ilse wished her to stay with Lucie while she confronted Hamid? Or telephoned the police?

She followed Dr. Ilse through the scented garden. "I heard noises and thought it was a burglar. When I realized he was in my office I knew at once it would be Hamid. He knows his way around my house. He used to be my patient, and for some time now he's been . . . "

Jocelyn had been listening with such concentration her ears rang. Now she stopped, because Dr. Ilse had stopped, and she followed Dr. Ilse's shocked gaze to the clothesline before them.

Hanging from it, illuminated in the cool of early dawn, was the one pretty set of underwear Jocelyn owned — the set she had found missing earlier the day before. If that wasn't odd enough, beside it was a brassiere she knew intimately, not because it was her own, but because it was the principal subject of the first still life she had done at the drawing studio with Monsieur Hamid. Rose-coloured, and constructed entirely of lace and intricate bands of ribbon, it must have cost a thousand francs.

"Silly Jimeta," Dr. Ilse murmured. "That pink one is mine. But *those* . . . " Dr. Ilse sat Lucie down on a garden chair and strode up to unpin Jocelyn's best set of underclothes.

"They're mine," Jocelyn said miserably, reaching to take them. She stuffed them in the pocket of her robe and hurried after Dr. Ilse.

They found Hamid on his knees scrabbling through the boxloads of files he had pulled from the floor-to-ceiling shelves. Papers flew through his hands with a speed that suggested he was not scanning the contents but waiting for a particular light to strike him from somewhere among Dr. Ilse's notes.

He made a growling sound that might have been directed at them as they stood in the doorway, but he did not interrupt his search.

"I've told him his file isn't here!" Dr. Ilse said.

When all but the top shelf of files was overturned on the carpet, it seemed to occur to the old man — for suddenly that was all he was — that Dr. Ilse might be of help.

"Where is it?" he said stupidly.

"Oh, Hamid — I moved all the old files to the clinic. . . . I was running out of room here . . . "

Hamid stood. His curled lip showed he did not believe her. "I'm parked on the street," he said, brushing off his pants. "Let's go." He had not glanced at Jocelyn.

Monsieur Hamid's vandalism gave Jocelyn something to talk about with Dr. Ilse when she ran into her in the street, and she took up the psychiatrist's invitation to join them for a Saturday picnic at the park. Dr. Ilse brought a refreshing *salade aux tomates*, and after they had eaten Lucie was happy to play a hiding game with the cats. "Have you seen the old woman who feeds all these cats?" asked Dr. Ilse.

Jocelyn nodded. The woman frightened her, because she seemed to need no one, no human, anyway. She treated the cats as if they were her children, her companions, her relations. If Jocelyn spent another ten or twenty celibate years, would she too begin to spend all her time feeding stray animals?

Dr. Ilse might have been reading her thoughts. "Men have always been my weakness," she said. Together they watched the old woman stoop beside the lower bushes, spreading her scraps of food. "But how can I regret my weakness?" Dr. Ilse added, smiling at her sturdy daughter, who had managed to pinch the tail of one of the cats and now whirled around with a great shout.

"Bravo, Lucie!" Jocelyn swung the little girl in the air to make her laugh.

"I can't regret it," Dr. Ilse went on. "But Jocelyn, you must know that there are those who seek not to create but to destroy. My stepson is jealous of his father the great artist, and so he tries to protect me. A truly Oedipal son, trying to murder out of love . . . "

Jocelyn pointed out that, as far as she could see, it was Hamid who was acting crazy. What was *his* complex?

Dr. Ilse laughed and shook her head. They watched Lucie run off to a striped cat that stood like a target, its tail switching, against a bush. Jocelyn felt a sudden chill. What had any of this to do with her?

"It could also be that Hamid is competing in a sexual way for me with my stepson Thierry . . . " murmured Dr. Ilse.

"But Thierry has a girlfriend . . . I told you about the girl in my class . . . she's very beautiful . . . " Jocelyn stopped, because now Dr. Ilse was really laughing. "Tell me what it's about," Jocelyn said quietly.

"It's not so dramatic." But the story began years before, when Hamid had come to Dr. Ilse because he worried that his interest in undergarments — greater than in the models who wore them — was abnormal.

"I told him it was his profession — he had artistic licence to draw what he pleased. But since he had to make money . . . " Dr. Ilse shrugged.

At that time, the art world showed absolutely no interest in Hamid's work. His still lifes of undergarments weren't seen as erotic or even pornographic. They were dismissed without discussion as odd and probably subversive, but of no more interest than the work of a student. So the first problem became financial: no one bought Hamid's drawings. Soon his gallery dropped him.

In therapy Hamid realized that he needed to make clearer the link he saw between his still lifes and western culture as a whole. Meantime he reached another, even more immediate crisis: he could not get new underwear to draw, and, Dr. Ilse added, he was no more able to draw the same garments over and over than he would have been to wear the same unlaundered pair of shorts each day. She suggested he buy his still life underclothing from the boutiques or the department stores, but for Hamid that was out of the question. He would not tolerate a store clerk's mistaken indulgence. Besides, what could be bought in the stores but bland, unoriginal reproductions designed with functionality in mind? In order to be interesting, Hamid maintained, an undergarment had first to be worn. To carry the idea further, an undergarment didn't truly become an undergarment until something had been worn *over* it.

The undergarments had to come from a private collection.

During his fourth year of spying and stealing, Hamid was arrested and, in lieu of a prison sentence, given a volunteer teaching task at an art studio. He was also required to continue psychotherapy.

This was his history, Dr. Ilse said simply. But seven years is a long time for a psychiatrist to spend with the same patient. It is a longer time than some people spend sharing intimacies with another person in their life.

Was he cured? Jocelyn asked.

Cured. . . . There was a shift, Ilse said, pausing to snuggle Lucie up in the blanket they had brought. After seven years of therapy Hamid no longer had the need to draw undergarments. And, she added almost as an afterthought, shortly after the formal conclusion of therapy, he and she became lovers.

Jocelyn nodded. There was still a chance for this to turn into a fairy tale.

But soon after they discovered they were going to have a child, Hamid had a distressing recurrence of his old symptoms.

It began with his demand to see Ilse's underwear; this time, when she refused, she could not do it on so-called professional grounds — "I could not refer to the normal doctor-patient relationship" — because she was no longer Hamid's psychiatrist. And there was something more disturbing.

As his psychiatrist she had done her best to keep her personal feelings out of the therapy. But now there was no protective professional screen. "I must have shown him my true feelings about his obsession. I must have let him know that, as a human being, I was revolted."

Enraged by her refusal and by his own shame, Hamid began once again to steal. This time he didn't bother with precautions. He quickly worked his way through working-class neighbourhoods, ripping brassieres and panties from the lines strung between windows while families sat eating their *côtelettes* and their *pâtes.* While the sun was still up he climbed over chipped-glass walls into high-class gardens.

He was ambitious, Dr. Ilse said, nodding as she remembered. Her tone was admiring. Hamid had wanted to show her his collection. Soon he had more undergarments than he could ever draw in a lifetime. He began to spend his time sorting and arranging them — here Dr. Ilse gestured with her hand — the usual thing artists end up doing to justify their periods of so-called unproductive thought. But he was also like the miser with his gold coins. No arrangement was good enough to draw, but he could never throw it out and start fresh.

But why undergarments, Jocelyn asked.

There was a silence, as if Dr. Ilse had not understood the question.

"Why brassieres and underwear and not, say, the body itself? The woman's body? Or flowers, or vegetables, or sunsets? Why was he obsessed with undergarments?"

"Obsessed? Perhaps we never know," Dr. Ilse said, stroking her sleeping daughter's hair. "There are of course theories, most of them motivated by political persuasion. But even after years of analysis, certain mysteries aren't to be solved. In fact they may serve to keep the analyst and the patient from looking at more important areas."

She smiled gently, and Jocelyn shook her head, exhausted by the weight of what she had been told. Did anyone know the labour of a psychiatrist? Dr. Ilse had begun to shiver, and for the first time Jocelyn understood the shivering to be an expression of the doctor's own fatigue.

"As a younger man Hamid was extremely attractive. Only in the past few years has he begun to fuss and pace like an old woman. And he used to smoke. Not that the smoking made him sexy. Or perhaps it did . . . " Dr. Ilse seemed lost. Jocelyn suggested they take Lucie home. Perhaps if the weather held for another day, Jocelyn could come by to take Lucie to the beach?

Jocelyn had begun to feel a connection with Dr. Ilse and Lucie. In spite of an attack of insomnia that had kept her almost entirely from sleep, she must have slept in the early morning, because she came to in a drowsy state in which the dogs were brawling and the neighbour was shouting at them and banging at the wall to get them to stop. And someone was banging at her door. It turned out to be Lucie, all ready with her pail and shovel and snack to go to the beach. Following behind with a wicker basket was Dr. Ilse.

With the hot sun sparkling and Lucie shrieking, Jocelyn forgot the fact that she could not have had more than a few hours' sleep. From the beach they strolled to a terrace café and ordered ices, and while Lucie babbled and played with her collection of animal cards, Jocelyn asked Dr. Ilse more about Hamid. Why had he wanted his file so badly that he risked another arrest breaking into her office?

"I imagine a certain life event was triggering feelings of panic. It seems someone in his class — your drawing class — someone knew where he got the undergarments for the still life arrangements and was threatening to ridicule him. This is all he would tell me. Of course it makes almost no sense."

But Dr. Ilse tried to articulate the syndrome she believed had made Hamid regress into stealing underwear from her clothesline. The fact that his habit had been discovered triggered helpless childish feelings of shame. No longer able to make rational choices, he was literally trapped in his worst period of weakness. "Given the deep layers of human emotion, what's surprising to me is that more of us don't behave this way," Dr. Ilse concluded.

She could have found a polite, professional reason to change the subject, but clearly she needed to talk. "You listen so well," she teased Jocelyn. "You ought to train as a psychiatrist."

Jocelyn stared. Dr. Ilse had undergone a sudden metamorphosis. Where she had been a large, buxom woman, a northern type used to a rugged life, her glance firm, her mouth wide and trusting, her hair shining with health — suddenly she looked ordinary. No, weaker than ordinary: she looked frail, as if anything that might happen could hurt her, even destroy her.

A few days later Dr. Ilse gave Hamid a photocopy of his entire file. "It isn't the usual procedure," she admitted. For days, Hamid and his weakness dominated discussions between Jocelyn and Dr. Ilse. With the second and last week of the summer drawing studio nearly over, it seemed Hamid was once again trying to come to terms with his anxiety. He asked to start therapy for the third time with Dr. Ilse.

Of course she refused. "As I should have done years ago, when he continually missed sessions . . . came late . . . threw tantrums," Dr. Ilse confided. "But at that time I couldn't close my door to him."

On the last day of class, most of the students were making only a show of setting up and painting the now-banal still lifes. Nathalia gazed into space and appeared to be thinking of nothing. Her sketching had not improved. The entire class had fallen into a trance. From the easels of the few students who continued to pull their Conté crayons across their papers, there rose a whispering, gritty sound. The whole studio was sighing with abandonment. Monsieur Hamid called for a long break well before the customary time.

Jocelyn bought fruit, and as usual returned earlier than the other students. She always liked to glance at everyone's work before the end of the break. But today the door was barred from the inside.

"I'm not ready." It was Nathalia's voice.

Ready? An odd thing to say, but then, Nathalia was an odd girl. Beautiful girls often were. But thinking this did not prepare Jocelyn for the spectacle she saw when Nathalia opened the door. Nathalia stood alone, nude, on the model's platform in the pose of a *portemanteau*. Instead of coats, her arms were hung with brassieres and panties, and to Jocelyn's horror she saw that they were all her own: the plain ones, the ones accidentally turned grey in the wash. The ones she hadn't even noticed were missing.

"I wouldn't let the others see you like that if I were you," Jocelyn said.

Nathalia smiled prettily. "Maybe I don't want to be like you," she replied.

Jocelyn had an insight: Nathalia wasn't trying to ridicule Hamid, she was humiliating Jocelyn. And for no reason. For no reason at all. For a lark. But how had Nathalia come upon Jocelyn's undergarments? Was Hamid stealing from Dr. Ilse *and* from Jocelyn? Was that why Jocelyn's one pretty set had gone missing and then reappeared on Dr. Ilse's line?

That would be too much, to have the old man collecting *her* old undergarments as well as Dr. Ilse's beautiful ones. Jocelyn felt a moment of acute and speechless anxiety, of not knowing, not understanding, and then, as if her feelings were mimicking the rise and fall of an ocean wave, she was flooded with the more pleasant, intellectual aspects of curiosity. What exactly was going through the beautiful Nathalia's mind? What was making her behave in just this way, and where might her actions lead? The best thing about feeling the entire curve of this intense curiosity was the sudden revelation it brought: Jocelyn was going to be a psychiatrist.

Everything was different. Everything was useful, everything was acceptable.

Many students had the habit of flipping their drawings over the tops of their easels before they left on break, but several had left theirs unturned. One had done a pale pencil drawing which altogether overlooked the presence of light and darkness. Another totally ignored the actual contours of the undergarments and had rendered them with crude symbolic shapes. Another, using charcoal, had left no lights at all, and the composition might have been of a dark wall. There was an ink wash which had destroyed several layers of newsprint, and an atmospheric chalk sketch in which nothing at all could be discerned. . . . Perhaps none of them were real artists, perhaps not one of them had any talent, but Jocelyn felt a sudden tenderness for them all. She was going to be a *psychiatrist*.

For the beautiful Nathalia, taking a course — whether in art or in accounting — was of little importance. For Jocelyn, taking courses had been a significant part of her life; around them she had squeezed in marketing, laundry and part-time jobs.

And for Hamid, teaching? From what Dr. Ilse had revealed, and with her own new-found psychiatric vision, Jocelyn could see that Hamid wanted much more than a pay cheque. More, even, than a chance to flirt with his son's girlfriend. It had to do with needing to publicly confess his secret obsessions, it had to do with lending them importance.

She did not take immediate notice of Nathalia, who was now walking in a slow circle around the easels, more nearly naked now that most of Jocelyn's homely undergarments had fallen to the floor.

But Nathalia seemed to hear her thoughts. "I like these courses," she said. "It's fun to meet a boy who isn't always travelling." And as Jocelyn was framing the sort of mild answer she thought a psychiatrist might give, and preparing her mouth to shape the words in a neutral way, she saw Thierry grind out his cigarette and enter the studio. And suddenly Jocelyn knew that Thierry was the missing piece.

From her personal point of view, things couldn't get any worse, but as a psychiatrist in training Jocelyn felt a new freedom from her own wishes and needs. She watched Thierry strut in front of Nathalia; she observed Nathalia's hair-tossing pretence of indifference.

Hamid returned, smelling of a foul herbal remedy. He seemed calm as he told Nathalia to get dressed before the other students came back. But Jocelyn saw him wipe at a trail of spit at the corner of his mouth. "Get dressed!" he barked. "*Petite idiote,*" he muttered, wiping his mouth again, as if he wished to erase even the memory of this disagreeable spectacle.

Jocelyn, meanwhile, was alert, rapturous. Didn't she know what many people struggled all their lives to know? Hadn't she discovered her calling? It did not occur to her that the faculty of medicine would reject her, considering her, at twenty-six, too old to begin the long course of studies. That the French, with all their reverence for the psyche, might put an age restriction on those permitted to study it did not enter her mind.

But Monsieur Hamid was standing beside her. Could he have a word with her? Yes, now, before the break was over? Throughout the drawing sessions he had been observing her. She showed unusual talent. His reference would not guarantee her entry into the École, but — and here he smiled coquettishly — it certainly couldn't harm her. In addition, it was in his capacity to invite her to sit for the admissions test.

"Oh. The admissions test," said Jocelyn, feeling small and clever and inarticulate. Abruptly her future as a psychiatrist dissolved. Of course she didn't want to listen to stupid Nathalia or obsessive Hamid. She wanted to make art. And she didn't want to listen to the arrogant Thierry in order to figure out his role in any Freudian complex, she just wanted to sleep with him.

She waited for Thierry that night in her kitchen with the light off. First she would catch him — stealing, replacing, whatever it was he came to do (and she couldn't have cared less which it was) — and then she would seduce him.

It was almost dark when he appeared. She saw him pin several undergarments to her section of clothesline. He didn't seem hurried — good for him, she thought, because he was going to be at her house for some time. He pinned up a long line of her own plain brassieres and underwear, the very ones Nathalia had posed with earlier. So, things *could* get worse, and worse yet. There was no end to shame. Jocelyn felt her breath full of self-hatred and imagined herself as a dragon, directing it outward. Then she forced herself to stop. She needed her energy to plan.

Call it rape. Would it be rape if he lay there, his penis limp? *Attempted* rape? This humiliating thought made her want to call off the seduction. Leave things to fate: end up, if she must, like the cat lady at the park. Or not: experience a miracle, Thierry turning, calling to her, My love, my love! She imagined herself gliding toward him at he stood on the walkway over the ravine. She was wearing something transparent and enveloped by a delicate perfume. She had just enough time to whisper his name before he crushed her in his arms . . .

Thierry stopped to examine the undergarments still draped over his arm. There was enough light from the moon to make out that they were not Jocelyn's. Indeed, they were far lacier and clearly much more expensive. Thierry entered Dr. Ilse's garden. A few moments later Jocelyn unlatched the gate and followed.

Dr. Ilse stood at her doorway in a long white wrap, something women had worn early in the century, in the age of psychoanalysis. It was she who held Thierry in her arms.

Jocelyn told herself she was not spying on the mother and stepson in their sad embrace; she was watching because she was curious to know what Thierry would do with all the lacy undergarments. By now they must be bunched against his chest.

It might have been a hallucination; she saw him drop a brassiere, but when she blinked it was still there between them.

Jocelyn understood much more than she wanted to about Dr. Ilse and Thierry from the way they stood in the soft evening light. She returned to her kitchen, switched on the light and stared at the cream-coloured paper on her easel. It reflected her own misery. The worst was that even if she did attack it with a pencil, or a piece of charcoal, none of the marks would have anything to do with her.

She could not get rid of the image of Dr. Ilse and Thierry, and so, when Jérôme returned from Salzburg later that night, she lit a candle and coaxed him to her bed. Since Jérôme had been burying cable close to her birthplace, she reasoned that he — and his semen — were in some way already connected to her and her world. She went to sleep immediately afterward, and the next day Jérôme thanked her and told her their love-making had helped him forget the exhaustion of his journey.

SPIES

It looked like this time he really had thrown her out the window. She wasn't buttering toast; she wasn't there to turn on the oven and open it a crack so they could lean over it eating their toast and not freeze. Dad didn't like the heat turned up.

One time Esmée thought he had thrown her out the window — she heard the glass — but in the morning there she was buttering toast with white margarine. She'd left it on the stove to soften and now she could cream in the orange powder. Perhaps she did all this so it wouldn't look like lard, which no one would want to eat, or worse, they would mix it up with lard and eat the lard instead. There were things Esmée's mother wanted kept secret; you could tell by the way she threw the cutlery in the drawer when Esmée asked her questions.

The time Esmée heard glass she didn't ask anyone about it, not even her brother Philip, but the next morning she went outside and poked around in the dirt below their bedroom window. No blood, no glass, nothing but the same tidy row of lily-of-the-valley, the sturdy flower-cups smelling like the Little Lady perfume Esmée wished she would get on her birthday the way her friends did.

She knew not to ask how her mother had survived the fall or how they got it all cleaned up and where they got the new window. That would be like asking someone why she wasn't dead.

But this time he had done it, he had killed her. All these years had been practice. Esmée had heard a creaking that meant Phil was out in the hall, and she met him at the top of the stairs and asked him what he was going to do. He showed her his jackknife, but there weren't any screams or thuds after that. They stood in the dark listening, and she supposed Phil wasn't sure of himself, because eventually he told her to go back to her room and she heard him going back to his own.

She might have slept. It was starting to get light when she heard the screen door. She knew it wasn't her father taking her mother out to the garage to beat her there so they wouldn't hear, because next she heard the car crackling out the driveway. She watched the taillights all the way down the avenue. They winked between the piles of snow that were shot through with pee and grit in the daytime but rose up spooky and majestic at night.

He was taking her to the hospital. He was going to pretend he didn't think she was dead; he would make them think he was trying to save her.

Esmée thought she should do something to mark this day — take her calendar and mark it with a black cross, or read a poem out the window, or say the Lord's Prayer and the Twenty-third Psalm. She fell asleep.

Morning came in spite of her mother's being dead, and now her father was making breakfast. All he had to do was add a bit of water and heat up the porridge; their mother always started it the night before. But he didn't know about adding the water and he was burning it.

"Esmée, you stir this while I get the toast going, that's a girl," he said.

Esmée was careful not to let her fingers touch his as she took the wooden spoon. The porridge was black on the bottom and they would have to eat it because now that he'd killed her he wouldn't leave for work while they were still eating, he would wait to make sure they finished and drank their milk. He was going to be there all the time now, at every meal. He would make sure they didn't try to fool him by flushing things like scrambled eggs (Phil) or turkey vegetable soup (Esmée) down the toilet.

When it was time to go to school Phil came into her room — something he never did — and told her to hurry up. As soon as they were in the alley Phil turned to cut through the neighbour's. "You go on. I'm taking a shortcut," he said.

Esmée knew the shortcut was the park, but she couldn't go with him; it would be her and a lot of high school boys laughing at her, standing around smoking dope.

"Are you going to skip school?"

"I might."

"Well, you better not go back to the house. He might go home before lunch."

"Then he'll get a surprise," Phil said.

At lunch Esmée knew she was home first because hers were the only tracks up to the porch. She was about to walk back down the alley to meet Phil when her father opened the door. "C'mon in, Ezie, it's cold out there," he said. "I'm just heating up some soup."

Esmée would throw up if he made her eat that turkey soup, but it turned out he hadn't got it out of the freezer, probably he didn't know it was there; he had opened a can of tomato soup. He broke crackers into his and spooned them into his mouth while they were still crunchy. He smelled of aftershave and hair tonic. The way his black hair was combed straight back with all that tonic made Esmée sick. Her own hair was red and went out like a red broom where it hit her neck, but at least she didn't oil it down. Also his nose was shiny and had blackhead holes without the blackheads. Esmée was going to get those if she kept squeezing. She wiped at her nose with her finger and it didn't come away greasy; that was good, the Ten-O-Six was working. And it was good for drying out pimples; the one she had picked until it bled was now an area of small scabs that came off easily.

"Don't pick at your face. Where's your brother, do you know, Ez?"

No, she didn't know, she told her father. She was so worried that she was eating her soup and drinking her milk and she couldn't tell the difference, whereas usually the milk made her gag because it wasn't real milk but powdered and had a blue tint that made you think of fish, or shark guts.

Then her father said, "I don't know if your mother ever wanted to be a wife and mother," but then, miraculously, Philip walked in, red-nosed and thin and hurrying to pull off his mitts and coat so he could blow his nose and wipe off his glasses. Their father asked him if it was still as cold out, and did Phil have schoolwork he had to stay to do, was that why he was so late? Phil was having trouble pulling off his mitts and Esmée prayed he hadn't done drugs, today of all days.

Then her father wanted to know when report cards were coming out, wasn't it soon?

Phil said he didn't think so, and Esmée knew her father was about to say that that wasn't good enough, that Phil should know when the reports were going to come out and be ready. But her father was looking at Phil in a funny way, as if they were at the A&W and instead of root beers Phil had brought them a tray full of banana splits nobody had ordered but her father didn't want to be rude because it was busy and the kid was obviously new.

"Well, sit down, son, and get some soup into you, maybe Ezie could make you some toast there, Ezie put in some more toast for your brother." Then her father pushed back his chair and told them he was going to lie down for half an hour before he had to go back to work.

Phil and Esmée started to whisper as if he'd bugged the kitchen. They got the dishes cleaned up and went upstairs, stepping around the creaks the way they always did when he was beating her and they had to go to the bathroom. They stood together brushing their teeth. You would never expect to brush your teeth in exactly the same way when your mother was dead and yet there they were, spitting and rinsing, and Esmée couldn't help the little feeling of pleasure she got running her tongue along her smooth fresh teeth.

Block H was science, and Mr. Hill gave Esmée two warnings but no detention, so she had to go right home after school. Phil was already there, standing in the window watching for her, and he came out to tell her to come in the front. He was watching cartoons on *Fun-O-Rama*. He wouldn't let her leave the living room, not even to go into the dining room.

"I don't want the cat to go all over the house," he said.

"What cat?" Esmée said, and Phil unzipped the hockey bag he'd put on the rocking chair. It was the cat that lived in the alley. It showed up as a kitten that summer and they gave it hamburger and chunks of cheese. Esmée had stopped petting it because it looked sick. Now its eyes were bright pinpoints. Phil pushed the rocker and the cat's mouth opened in a soundless growl.

"Why'd you bring it home?"

"Why not? 'Come in out of the cold — get in here,' isn't that what Dad says? I'm doing him a favour." Phil pushed the rocker again and the cat whined.

"Don't, he doesn't like that. Who're you doing a favour, the cat?"

"That's right."

They stood over the cat, not petting it, and then Esmée knew Philip had done something to it. "You made it smoke dope," she cried.

Philip snorted.

"Well, you gave it drugs."

Phil took out a string and dangled it over the cat. The cat squirmed and made its wretched howl.

"You tied it up!"

Phil was looking through the TV guide. "*The Spy Who Came In From the Cold*. This is for you, kitty. I gave it a tab of psilocybin a few minutes before you came home, Ez, it should be wild by the time Dad gets home. Now I have to do its claws."

"Jesus. What are you going to do to his claws?"

"Paint them."

Phil put on gardening gloves and took the cat's paws. He tied them together with a strip of bedsheet so they were splinted straight out in front. "So he doesn't lick them." He took a bottle from his pocket and a paintbrush. "Curare. Pretty deadly. It comes from Peru."

"Where'd you get that brush? That's my brush," Esmée said.

Phil painted the cat's claws with the resinous solution. On TV Richard Burton was kissing a brunette whose side-parted hair fell over one eye in just the way Esmée wished hers would.

"Is she a spy?" Esmée asked.

"No! He lives at her house. Come on." Phil carried the hockey bag with the cat in it to the kitchen. "Okay, kitty, you're going to have to use your night vision now," he said. He opened the cupboard over the sink and lifted the cat out of the bag. He bound the cat against the back of the cupboard with a strip of sheet and worked the ends of the sheet through slits at the sides. "I filed these," he said, showing Esmée the gap between the back and sides of the cupboard. "When I give you the signal, you climb up on the counter and lean around and cut the knot. The scissors are up here. Dad will think you're looking for the baking soda."

"Why would I be?"

"To put out the fire."

After he'd tied the cat in the cupboard Phil let Esmée go to the bathroom and up to her room. She came down with her oil paints and a bag of cloth scraps she used to sew doll clothes.

"You don't need all that. We're not going camping," Phil said. "That's Richard Burton."

"As if I didn't know."

At the commercial Phil went to the bathroom and Esmée changed the channel to *Where the Action Is*.

"What'd you do?" he said when he came back. He switched it back to the movie.

"Which one is the spy?"

"They're both spies."

"But for different sides?"

"The German's working for a British guy in Germany. Shh."

At the next commercial Phil explained. "There's a spy in the British organization in England who doesn't actually exist."

"What do you mean?"

"Well, he may or he may not."

"Be dead?"

"No!"

Richard Burton was walking in the rain with the German girl.

"But is the German girl a spy?"

"Yeah, she hides an Uzi under her apron."

Esmée set up her jars to do a new paint-by-number.

"See, Burton's posing as a writer."

"Who's that German guy?"

"A colonel, but on the British side, that's why he let Burton go."

"Why doesn't he let the other guy go?"

"Because he knows too much. Pay attention."

"I am."

Burton was helping the girl over the Berlin wall. There was gunfire and the girl fell in a heap. Esmée turned back to her blank paint-by-number. She felt the grainy surface of the canvas. It was textured to look like cloth. When she looked up again they were showing the credits.

"So what happens to Richard Burton?" Esmée was thinking about the girl but she knew better than to ask.

"He goes back to England a wreck, with the job well done."

It was past six, and their father always got home at six. From her place on the couch Esmée would see him if he walked up the front stairs, but he would come in the back from the garage.

"The cat's going to be nuts," Phil said. "Wherever it scratches him he'll seize up," Phil said. "And I've only got my learner's. He might not make it to the hospital."

"Is that why the cat's in a splint — so that it can't lick its paws?"

But Phil was concentrating on the commercial.

"We could call a taxi. Or the ambulance."

"Who could, you?"

"No." Esmée was not sure he heard her quiet voice.

Around seven Phil was hungry. "Aren't you hungry?" he said.

Esmée didn't know. Sometimes she thought she was hungry but when she started eating she felt like throwing up. Other times the smell of someone's salt and vinegar chips from the machine at school made her feel sick, but if she ate one she would wish she had money to buy her own.

It was past eight when their father came home. He stood in the dining room doorway. "It's cold out there," he said. "Your mother needs to rest a while longer. I could use some rest myself. How about some scrambled eggs, could you help with that Ezie, that would hit the spot." Then he went upstairs to change.

Phil and Esmée stayed frozen for a moment and then Phil went to the kitchen and poured half a bottle of cooking oil down around the large element.

Their father came back with his tie off and he rolled up his sleeves and told Esmée he could take over there if she wanted to start the toast. He was using a metal fork to scramble the eggs on the Teflon pan but Esmée didn't say anything. She kept her eye on him while she got bread from the freezer and sure enough, he was shaking pepper into the eggs when the element burst into flames.

"Get the baking soda!" Phil cried.

Esmée pulled herself up onto the counter and got the scissors. She had to feel behind the cupboard for the sheet. Phil and her father were yanking open the drawers and cupboards.

"What the hell are you doing, Ez?" her father said.

"It's in here," Esmée said. She hacked away at the sheet. Finally she got it cut and then she cried out, "It's jammed!" as if she'd been trying to open the cupboard.

Her father pushed her out of the way. He pulled out all the cans and when he got the baking soda he was shaking it before he got to the stove. The air was full of powder. Then the flames were suffocated and it was all over.

"Lord almighty," he said.

He got a rag and wiped at the mess until the rag was moving it around like finger paint. He scraped the blackened egg into the garbage. "Maybe we'll have crackers and cheese," he said. "Have we got any of that sharp cheddar? Lordy, what a smell. Is that from the fire?"

Esmée knew it wasn't. The smell of throw-up was coming from the cupboard. Her father went to it and fished around.

"Oh, Christ," he said, pulling out the cat. "Christ almighty."

His face was hidden while he washed his hands in the sink. He took a long time, and then he went to the back door and put on his coat. "I'm going to swing over to the hospital," he said. "You have this cleaned up before I get back or you won't be able to sit down for a week. The both of you."

They watched him close the door and then Phil turned and went upstairs. Esmée knew he'd gone to smoke out his window.

Esmée felt numb from her chin down. She put the cat in an old grocery bag and pulled on her boots and without bothering with her coat and mitts she went out into the alley. She couldn't think what to do with the cat. The ground would be too hard to dig into, and if she buried the cat in the snow it would be there in the spring. She stood a moment under the stars, and then she heard a door slam and thought she had better start walking. When she came to the road she crossed it and went on to the next alley. She was thinking she could do this forever; she would never have to go back or go anywhere or do anything, it would be like being dead. But eventually she came to the cloverleaf. There were no more alleys.

"Okay, kitty," she said. "Out you go." She held up the bag and slid the cat out gently. She reached down and unthreaded the strip of sheet from around its paws. "You're a nice kitty. I wish you could have got away," she said, but she was thinking maybe it wouldn't have made any difference if she had been quicker to cut the knot behind the cupboard. Maybe the cat had already breathed in fumes from its claws or gone crazy on the drug. Maybe psilocybin could give a cat a heart attack; maybe it had already thrown up and died when Phil gave her the signal to cut it loose.

She felt the small pads under each paw and then she buried her face in the cat's fur. Out in the cold it didn't smell bad and if she got a disease from it, that was fine, that was just fine with her. She sat in the snowbank stroking the cat, and she stayed there until she knew her fingers were going to get frostbitten. If she had to be alive she wanted to have her fingers; she knew that. She made a snow blanket for the cat, and then she stood. There was still the bag. She threw it into the air, and she watched the wind catch it and carry it over toward the middle of the cloverleaf, and then she turned back into the alley.

SLEEPING WITH THE INSANE

When Olwyn whispered that she knew how to do something with a photograph to make Brian like Cassie again, Cassie didn't look up from the coffin and she didn't answer. It was Olwyn's father who had died — he'd had a heart attack and fallen down the stairs, was what the other kids were saying. Cassie just stared down at the dirt and the flowers Olwyn and her mother had thrown in, because she thought it was wrong to stand at someone's open grave talking about boys or worrying, as she was, about Tricia Berg, who on the walk over from Olwyn's said that Cassie's hair wasn't blonde at all but brown, light brown. Brian probably wanted to go out with Tricia Berg now. All the boys did.

Cassie could see no reason for Olwyn's wanting to help her get Brian back. She and Olwyn weren't close; they just happened to be standing beside each other at the grave. Once in grade four Cassie went over to Olwyn's to play Barbies and Olwyn brought out a box of Kotex instead, real ones. "Do you want to play Kotex?" Olwyn said with her smirky look. Olwyn had kept that smirky, sulky look, as if she was just waiting for you to turn her in, and not surprisingly none of the teachers liked her, even in high school, where you had better odds.

Cassie glanced over at her. Nearly all the other kids, the girls anyway, were crying, but Olwyn wasn't, and it was her father. Olwyn was taller than most of the boys and she let her dark hair hang straight down so that her ears stuck out. Why didn't she just put all her hair behind her ears? She was definitely not crying, and she was doing that thing with her fingers, rubbing them like a rat cleaning its paws.

I don't think I met Olwyn.

Cassie had no feelings for Olwyn's father, but she was sniffling anyway because she didn't have a jacket and the drizzle had turned cold and windy. She tried to pretend it was her own father who had died but she hadn't seen him for years and she didn't know how old-looking to make him. It was easier to think of her mother, not dying but packing to leave. Her mother's dresser drawers were open and she was refolding the orlon sweater with the appliquéed pink and mauve leaves. Then she changed her mind and threw it on the floor because Cassie had given it to her, and she packed just her old fisherman knit cardigan — shrunk short and bunchy even though she was the one who had washed it. She stuffed her underwear and stockings in the side pockets and clicked everything shut. Then she bumped her suitcase down the back stairs, and halfway down, remembering, she turned to throw the house keys up at Cassie. She lurched off in her powder blue Valiant, spitting gravel into a cloud of dust. By the sink she'd left a twenty-dollar bill held down by a can of Chunky Manhandler Stew. It was all because Cassie was selfish.

I was sometimes afraid of her imagination.

Thinking about this made Cassie feel the way she imagined you would if you held dry ice against your breasts.

Olwyn's father may have been drunk. Got drunk, fell down the stairs, had a heart attack. Or he wasn't drunk, but had a heart attack anyway and fell down the stairs. Or he was drunk and had a heart attack at the top of the stairs, which made him fall. Cassie had not asked Olwyn. Olwyn was probably in shock. That was why she wasn't crying, and why she had just said the thing about Brian. Since she was already beside her, Cassie walked with her to the cars. Olwyn had a long stride; the others followed far behind in a sort of rock-festival wave.

Olwyn was still rubbing her fingers. This was the sort of thing she did that revealed to Cassie that they would never be friends and certainly never best friends. The drizzle was turning to rain. The dirt would be mud before the gravediggers got the grass down.

"You still like him, don't you? You should have a party. Soon, so you'll be together for camping. You just have to get a photograph of him. Do you like him because he looks like Jim Morrison?"

"Not really." Olwyn thought she knew all about Brian, but she didn't, she didn't know any more than any of the other girls knew from lying on Olwyn's bed drinking lemon gin.

Cassie's mother's bedroom door was shut when she got home. She took a bowl of yoghurt and jam up to her attic room and sat under the covers reading a pamphlet on contraception. The house was quiet when she went down to get more yoghurt. Even before her brother had left Cassie had taken food to her room instead of eating meals with him and her mother.

She put the bowl on the floor and snuggled down, imagining she was at a party with Brian. They were lying on a couch, the way they had in grade nine, when he first moved out from Burnaby. Then she pretended Brian was in her room, and she felt her stomach fall, and she imagined them kissing, and the outdoor smell of his shirt and hair, and then she touched herself and pretended they had taken off their clothes.

She had one boyfriend who winked at me.

She woke in the night because her mother was making a terrible noise in the kitchen. There was no point thinking about Brian. Even if they got Brian to like her again, there was still her mother. What was she doing? Something with the cutlery. Perhaps she was finding forks that Cassie had not washed properly.

I don't remember meeting Brian.

In the morning it was still raining, and her mother's door was shut again. Cassie got food quietly, and before noon she left a note by the sink and walked across the fields and through the town to Olwyn's. The kids were upstairs watching an old war movie. It would have been offensive to smoke up in the basement and listen to Zeppelin so soon after the funeral. There was a damp smell of socks and jeans mixed in with the cigarette smoke, and as usual the windows were closed. The kids lay fan-shaped in front of the television. Olwyn's mother's yellow knitting was folded on her chair; perhaps she was in her bedroom having a drink. Richard was in Olwyn's father's La-Z-Boy; Tricia was leaning against his legs, helping him pass the beer he was sharing with LeDrew, who had the couch to himself. As soon as she found a place on the rug Cassie wanted to leave again.

I never met Olwyn.

Cassie found Olwyn washing the already clean kitchen floor. "I'd better stay here with my mom," Olwyn said, as if Cassie had asked her to go somewhere.

They decided that the first good day they would try out Olwyn's tent and have a party at Cassie's. Cassie watched Olwyn swish the rag in the bucket, wring it out, and start on a new place. She could have been writing her lover's name beside her own on the sand. Cassie wanted to feel sympathy for her; there was no reason Olwyn should have no one to dream about when she lay in her bed.

Cassie never washed the floor at home. The first time her mother went into the hospital, the note had said she would be home by the weekend. Cassie had worked the J-Cloth into a fine point and got every bit of grease from the knobs on the stove clock that didn't work. She hugged the toilet to get at the back. Used a fork to dig out the dustballs behind the fridge. Scoured the fridge with Comet until she saw it was lifting off the last bit of sheen. The next day her aunt drove out with chili and told them their mother was in the psychiatric ward. Cassie felt crazy herself, so she wasn't surprised. "It's hereditary, isn't it," she said. Her aunt told them their mother was just depressed. But Cassie stopped cleaning. What was the point of trying to get the attention of a depressed lunatic?

When she was little she was my sunshine.

It stopped raining on Saturday morning. By noon it was hot, and Olwyn called to say she could bring the tent if Cassie came to help carry it. Cassie went to ask, but her mother's door was shut. She stretched the telephone cord up the stairs to her room, and stepped from the top stair to the one below and back up again, thinking: She's depressed, she's not depressed, she's depressed, not depressed. "It should be okay to put the tent up," she told Olwyn. "I'll ask later about the party."

When they got back her mother's room was open, the bed unmade. There were several glasses of water on her night table. "Maybe she went out to buy aspirin," Olwyn said.

"We have lots." Cassie showed her the pills her mother kept in a Chinese lacquer box.

She lent Olwyn a bathing suit so they could tan. Olwyn groaned pulling it on. "I'm so fat," she said. She wasn't, but no matter which way she adjusted her breasts, they bulged out of Cassie's suit.

"It's just my suit. I'm flat-chested," Cassie said.

"No, yours are like in the ads!"

Cassie told her she was crazy. She hated her flat chest, her stomach that stuck out. The only part of her body she wouldn't change was her hands. Even there, she might make the fingers longer, tapered. Wasn't that what was pretty? Tapered fingers?

> She used to say she wished she was pretty. I didn't think men would want to be with a woman who thought too highly of herself.

They put the tent up at the edge of the field, as far from the house as possible, and Cassie squinted into the summer haze pretending she was homesteading with Brian. She brought down the blanket from her bed and spread it by the tent over the thick weeds. It was hot, and after a few minutes she ran back up to the house to get ice cubes. She wanted to check if her mother was working a shift, but she couldn't find her pocket calendar. The sudden cool of the house was dizzying and slightly creepy, as if there was a suffering animal in the basement. "Either she'll be home in a while and you can ask her then about the party or she's working and you won't have to," Olwyn said. Olwyn wanted Cassie to roll the ice cube across her back, and Cassie said all right, she had to say all right because she couldn't tell Olwyn the truth about her mother. That's what happened when you had something to hide: you ended up doing what everyone else wanted so they wouldn't find out your secret. She told herself it didn't matter as long as she just held the ice cube and didn't touch Olwyn's skin with her fingers. To touch someone that much you should at least like her. Then she felt guilty, because Olwyn offered to rub baby oil on her, and she rubbed it not just on her back, on the places Cassie couldn't reach herself, but down her front and legs. "You've got soft skin," Olwyn said, and "God, look how white it is under your bathing suit," and "I'll put some under your arms for when you turn over." Cassie kept her eyes closed, and she felt Olwyn's fingers slide over her nipple, just once, so that it nearly didn't happen. Then she heard her snap on the top of the baby oil.

Sometimes I was afraid of her imagination.

At three-thirty, her mother still wasn't home. Cassie got a headache from the sun and took three aspirin. They threw the blanket in the tent and put on cut-offs to walk to the store to see if anyone knew where they could get a Polaroid camera. There were only younger kids sitting on their bikes in the gravel. These were the kids who hung out behind the video arcade at night with their glue-bags. Cassie and Olwyn got gum and licorice and started back. They were hanging over the bridge trying to see who was swimming in the creek when Gary Andreason pulled over. He wanted to know what they were up to. He always wanted to know that. Cassie said, "You should be a narc," but Olwyn was nicer. She asked if he was coming to the party and could he bring a Polaroid camera. Gary wanted to know what kind of party — an orgy? — and who all was invited. He was asking Olwyn because he knew Cassie didn't like him. She hoped he knew that. She had been trying to tell him since grade eight. She had liked him until he put his school photo in her back pocket.

"Just you, so far. Is that Brian Lester?" Olwyn pointed to the boy walking down to the creek.

"Yeah, I just dropped him off," Gary said. "Should I ask him?"

"Sure. Ask a few people," Olwyn said.

I never met Gary. I went steady with a nice young man before I was married. I guess he wasn't exciting enough for me.

Gary and Brian arrived first. Gary had Eddy Schuler's Polaroid; Eddy had gone into town to buy some dope. Cassie waited for a good moment to take a picture of Brian. He sat with the headphones on, eating Olwyn's potato salad and reading a record cover. Cassie finally took a picture of Gary standing at the fridge pretending he was about to drink milk straight from the carton. Then she told him to sit with Brian and Olwyn. She meant to get one of Brian by himself after that, but Gary grabbed the camera, and when he had taken a picture of Cassie, one of Cassie and Olwyn, and another one of Cassie, there was no more film.

"It doesn't matter," Olwyn said. She pulled Cassie into the bathroom and stood against the door because she knew the lock didn't work. "We can use any picture that's got Brian in it," she said. "Okay, now we need to get at least one of his hairs. And it would be great if we could get some spit and some nail clippings."

"Nail clippings?" Cassie was thinking of her brother, who used to clip his toenails while he watched TV.

"Well, nails are probably the hardest. Let's concentrate on his hair and spit for tonight. We can augment the charm later. When you get to know him," Olwyn said, and she went back out into the party.

Augment. Cassie had never heard anyone but her old piano teacher use that word. And she had no idea how to get some of Brian's spit. It turned out not to be that easy getting a hair, either. His jean jacket was on the back of the kitchen door, but there wasn't one hair on it. But it seemed Olwyn was having better luck. "I got one," she said. "Bring those empties." She disappeared again into the bathroom. Cassie followed, feeling self-conscious carrying the case. "Brian put his in that end, I was watching," Olwyn said. "But there are five. He probably only drank a couple. Well, it doesn't matter: if it's the wrong one the chemicals won't match up with his picture. I'm putting the hair here so watch it." Olwyn was talking like an expert. She moved the bar of soap and wiped the side of the sink clean so she could use it to mix the last drops of beer from each bottle.

"But why do you want the beer he drank?"

"Not the beer, the spittle. Spit, nail clippings, hair. They're all good. Obviously we can't just tell him to spit, but the liquid beer is bound to catch whatever spit he put on the rim." She glanced at Cassie, and Cassie had the thought that Olwyn was probably the smartest girl she knew, but smart in a way that only made her life worse. Boys didn't like it and teachers didn't know about it because Olwyn was always skipping school, not so that she could perform experiments or read university books, the way you might expect someone really smart to do, but just to watch the soaps. Olwyn picked up the one hair. "Where'd you find it?" Cassie asked.

"I pulled it out," Olwyn said. "Got any tape?" Cassie shook her head, but Olwyn was already going through the medicine cabinet. "Ha," she said, holding up a single Band-Aid that had been sitting forever on the bottom shelf with the toothpaste, so that the wrapper was soaked through and greasy looking. Olwyn ripped the Band-Aid with her teeth and taped the one hair she'd got to the side of Brian's head in the photograph. "Okay, last thing," she said. "Your spit now, or better yet, get it from between your legs. I'll turn around." Olwyn turned her head. "You want me to try? Just kidding."

> I trusted her to choose good friends. I didn't meet Olwyn.

Cassie reached miserably down her cut-offs. Amazed, she brought out a wet finger.

"Got some? That'll do it," Olwyn said. "Okay, rub it along the edges of the photograph. Good. Now you've encircled him with your power of attraction. He will be miserable until he possesses you for his own."

"His own what?"

"His own. His girlfriend. Oh. And if he doesn't, you just bury the photograph and he will waste away."

"You mean he'll get sick?"

"Well. I think it must depend on his vulnerabilities. Does he have allergies?"

"I don't know."

"Well, anyway. You bury it in a spot where neither sun nor moon can shine on it," Olwyn said. "That's easy. That just means take it outside and dig a hole. But put it in a tin so the animals don't dig it up."

"Why don't I just put it in my desk drawer?" Cassie said.

"Whatever."

Brian was sitting on the counter. Olwyn held out one of the pictures that was just of her and Cassie. "What do you think?" she said. "Miss PNE Twins, huh?"

"Couple of pinheads," Brian said. He flipped his beer cap into the sink and went into the living room. Cassie could hear Tricia Berg in there giggling in a loud voice. In that instant Cassie knew there was no point thinking about Brian. She had always known but now she had to stop pretending. Also, she was going to stop pretending she didn't know where her mother was. At that precise moment she was probably in the lounge, huddled over her coffee. She never took the mug far from her lips. She hated the smoke and the loud TV but she was smiling at everyone — even at the horrible, toothless men — and talking with them about their medications and their favourite programs, as if she were a visiting nurse.

They were the family I never had.

Cassie had the white pages open to the hospital listings when someone thought he heard knocking and opened the back door. It was the cowboy from the psych ward. When Cassie visited her mother that time the cowboy was sitting at a table under the television playing solitaire. Cassie was sure she wasn't the only one watching him instead of the TV, and it was no wonder: he looked exactly like her old TV hero, Jim, from *The Wild, Wild West*. He had the same tanned face, the pink lips, strong, steady hands. She called him the cowboy because he wore a gold string tie and an embroidered denim shirt with studs. Now he was wearing a not-so-new plaid shirt with the same string tie. He didn't look exactly like Jim in *The Wild, Wild West* any more but he still looked nice, in a beat-up way. He told Cassie he'd rather leave his boots outside because they had mud on them, and his voice was wonderfully deep and crumbly, and she was just nodding and nodding and couldn't say a thing. Olwyn was matter-of-fact. "Your pants, too," Olwyn said. Trust Olwyn to notice the dark streak across his jeans.

It seemed he was supposed to meet Cassie's mother for coffee. She must have thought it was a different day, he said. He didn't have anything else to do, so he thought he'd walk over. "I knew it was down from the OK Tire," he said. He was smiling, but Cassie could tell he felt uncomfortable with Zeppelin and a houseful of stoned kids.

Gary saved the day, introduced himself, found out the cowboy's name was Victor.

"Victor? Can I get you a beer?"

> Victor used to wink at me. He was broad-shouldered, more manly than her other boyfriends.

Victor took a long drink, as if he'd just done some hard work. Cassie saw Tricia Berg coming and she touched Victor's arm and asked him to come outside.

"We're camping out tonight," she said. She pointed down to the tent. Victor pushed the bag he had brought into the corner of the porch so there was room for them both to lean against the railing. There still wasn't much room, and Cassie noticed how cool the rail felt pressing against her stomach, while the place where Victor's leg touched hers was burning. "What's in the bag?" she said.

"A dead cat."

"Ha." She went to light a cigarette and Victor held his hand over the lighter and told her not to. Stunned, she put the cigarette back in the pack.

"Are you allergic to smoke?" she said.

"No. It would spoil the air," Victor said. "And what if I wanted to kiss you?"

"Ha."

Victor touched her cheek, turned her face to him. "Are you afraid I'm going to?" he said.

Cassie nodded.

"But you'd like me to?"

Cassie imagined that Victor was Dutch or Russian. He wanted to take her back to the country he loved.

"What's really in the bag?" she said.

"A dead cat. I told you."

Cassie wanted to laugh and laugh. She grabbed Victor's hand and they ran down the path by the potatoes to the end of the field and the ditch. On the way back Cassie stumbled in the mud, and Victor caught her.

"Perhaps you would like me to carry you," he said.

"No!" Cassie was limping. Laughing. They were at the tent now. "Do you know I called you the Cowboy?" she said.

"The Cowboy." Victor stopped. "And did you want to go into the tent with the Cowboy?"

Cassie nodded.

The next day she knew — and perhaps she knew even then, crouched inside the tent, holding the flap open for him — that Victor would have been the perfect first lover. They rolled from one side of the tent to the other, playing.

"The tent's going to collapse," Cassie said.

"You've got the hiccups," Victor said.

She knew from the way the gravel sounded at the road that her mother was home.

She told Victor, and when he didn't move, she pushed him off her and jumped out of the tent and ran up to the house. She would tell her mother Victor was out there to get away from the noise. (And he was.) But her mother didn't get out of the car. From her attic room Cassie watched Victor crawl out of the tent and straighten up. He walked straight into the path of the headlights and disappeared. Then her mother backed out of the driveway. Cassie went downstairs and told everyone to leave.

Brian was in her mother's room, sprawled on the bed. She stood over him, over his cute bum and legs in his boot-cut jeans, and she said in a loud voice that the party was over. She knelt by the bed. If she leaned forward she could kiss his cheek, there above the thin stubble. She wasn't going to. "What happened?" she said softly. "Huh? What happened to you?" She rocked on her heels and gave his shoulder a poke. It felt hard, and she wanted to lay her hand against it and dig her fingernails in. "Okay," she said. "Wake up." She slung his arm over her shoulder. There was no delicious sexy feeling in her stomach; it was more like having a vacuum cleaner hanging from her neck.

> I don't know why she's talking about vacuums. When did she ever vacuum the house?

In the kitchen a frizzy-haired boy who hung out in front of the café was ripping the skin off a sausage with his teeth. When he saw Cassie he used the sausage to flick back his hair. Cassie grabbed it and threw it in the sink. She could see Tricia Berg on the couch, laughing for no reason, throwing bits of fluff at Gary. Cassie made as much noise as she could collecting ashtrays and dishes, and then she went out and sat in the tent to wait for everyone to leave. She wasn't surprised when Gary followed her.

> Gary had broader shoulders than her other boyfriends. He used to wink at me.

"Is everyone gone?" she said.

"Pretty well." Gary told her there was some smoke, but Brian got it before it turned into a fire. "There's a small hole in the chair in your mother's room but you can't see it; it's under the cushion," he said. He asked if he could have one of the pictures with Cassie in it. Cassie said he could. (He could have the one that stank, if he wanted, but she didn't tell him that.)

"I was a bitch to kick everyone out, huh," she said.

Gary said it was late anyway. He offered to bring his brother's truck over if she needed anything. She said all right. It was cold now, and she wanted to get into her sleeping bag, but it looked like Gary was there to stay. There was really nothing wrong with him. She couldn't remember why she had stopped liking him in grade eight. "Did you know my mother was on the psych ward?" she said.

"I knew the other time. Is that where she is tonight?"

"Just to visit. You know, it's hereditary. I could be crazy without it showing yet."

"No, you couldn't." Gary moved closer. She knew he wanted to put his arm around her.

"Sure I could. You don't start off completely insane." She pushed by him and walked up to the house. It was possible, she was thinking, that Brian would be sobered up. He would be reading a magazine in the living room. He would be remembering all the things he had liked about her in grade nine. In that case he would be in for a big surprise.

> Wait now: it was Brian who liked to wink at me.

But her mother's room was empty. Brian was gone. Olwyn had the whole place cleaned up. "So Brian put out a fire," Cassie said.

"Well, I hope so. He started it," Olwyn said. "He was the only one in there." She had the kitchen cleaner than Cassie had ever seen it. There were roses floating in a cereal bowl; she must have picked them from the bushes out front. Olwyn and Cassie pulled the chair onto the porch to air it out.

"I hate houses that have couches and stuff on the porch," Cassie said. "It's like old cars you *know* nobody's going to fix." She was willing herself not to cry. "Oh. The Cowboy forgot his bag," she said. It was an ordinary garbage bag, not even half full. She picked it up to take it inside.

"What is it, clothes?" Olwyn said.

"I guess." But it was heavier, like sugar.

Years later a friend of Cassie's was working at Riverview and told her about a sweet man who liked to wear gold string ties. Cassie visited Victor, and he remembered her, and where she had lived down from the OK Tire Store, and her tent, but at first he didn't remember about the dead cat. They got it sorted out, though; he'd misunderstood at first, thought she wanted to know what that particular cat had looked like. "It was night time," Victor said. "But I do remember it was a big cat. That one I picked up along the Trunk Road. I had to chase it a ways. Where did you bury it?" He was interested, conversational.

"At the edge of the field," Cassie said. "Not that far from where we had the tent." Victor was happy with that, and he nodded his approval.

Cassie opened the bag, so she was the one who felt the fur and before she could get her hand out, the soft, livery flesh. Innards. She told herself this was why she let Olwyn hold her while she threw up, why she let her help her get cleaned up, walk her to the tent. Years later, it didn't seem that Olwyn should have been that much less upset, less needy.

The air in the tent was damp. Her breath still smelled of throw-up, so she was trying to face away from Olwyn. "Do you think I'm insane?" she said. It seemed natural not to talk about the dead cat.

> Oh yes, she used to ask me that. What should I have said? She had such an imagination.

"Not right now," she added. "But that I could be headed that way?"

"I wouldn't want to know if I was," Olwyn said. "Do you want me to give you a foot massage?"

"You don't have to." Cassie had never had a massage. She wasn't surprised when Olwyn went ahead and began to rub her neck. There were rustling, windy sounds outside the tent. Summer was going to be over. Olwyn's fingers were quick, but clingy; they zigzagged nervously across Cassie's cool throat and chest.

"They're like in the ads because they could fit into a champagne glass. See?" Olwyn cupped her hand over Cassie's breast. "I read that in *Elle*, that magazine." The hand moved down to her belly. Cassie was glad, furiously glad that Olwyn was doing this, because it kept her from thinking. She wasn't thinking about the cat or the Cowboy or her mother, she was thinking of nothing, nothing at all, when she breathed in the wrong way and choked. She had to cough, huddled over, until her stomach was sore. When she could breathe again she lay back, exhausted, and when she felt Olwyn's hand she flung it away.

> I didn't meet Olwyn.

"Do you want me to leave?" Olwyn asked. Cassie didn't answer. "I could go up to your house," Olwyn said. "I'd be right there."

"It's okay. It's your tent." Cassie was breathing all right now, and she was sinking into sleep, sinking past it even, deep into the cool ground. Nothing was important after all.

But then it was again. Before dawn she had a bad dream that woke her up crying so hard she got the hiccups again. She told Olwyn her dream, told her the bits she could remember — except the part about the Cowboy. She lay shivering in the near-light with the racket from the birds, telling Olwyn her dream without knowing if Olwyn was listening or even awake. Cassie finished telling the dream and still Olwyn said nothing. She thought Olwyn would put her arm out, touch her, perhaps touch her hair. It began to seem like hours that she waited, and what she couldn't understand was why, when the sun was coming up, it was just getting colder.

PHANTOM PAIN

Lise sat by her wide-open bedroom window watching people queue up for the tram that went straight down to the Grande Place in the heart of Brussels. Lise was waiting for a gap between people so she could spit, and while she waited she anchored her bubble gum between her front teeth and stretched it out with her fingers until it grew thin in the middle and broke. Then she chewed it back into a ball and began again. She had her spit ready and was holding the gum under her tongue. And although she would not have told you this or written it in her diary, Lise was also waiting for her father to finish with the girl in his third-floor *cabinet*.

Her father was a gynaecologist and he owned the third and fourth floors of the building. He liked to examine girls of thirteen and fourteen, not much older than Lise. But Lise never worried that he might tell her to come down to the third floor, because she looked exactly like her mother, who was always sick. It was nothing gynaecological, said her father. He touched his head. She was sick up here, and that was why she went twice a week to an analyst who was helping her to see that her pain was all made up.

Ian was the same age as Lise. He was growing up several zones back in time, in Montreal, and he knew nothing of analysis and quite a lot about real pain. By the time he was ten he had smashed himself against the boards at the hockey rink from every angle he could imagine.

"Ronny. Do you know what they had to do when my knee swoll up?" Ian was propped up on his good elbow so he could watch the snow falling against the streetlight. His younger brother Ronny did not answer, because he only wanted to go to sleep, but Ian told him anyway. He told Ronny how he had smashed his knee against the ice and had to glide off on one skate and it took half an hour before he was thawed enough to feel anything, but meanwhile his leg had swollen and they had to cut the seam of his pants to get them off.

Every night he focused on one part of his body and described the sensation of pain in vivid detail. After two or three of these stories on the same night Ronny told him to shut up, to just shut up, but Ian went on until he was too tired to hold himself up on his good elbow, and he had to talk with his head on the pillow and looking straight up at the ceiling. When he ran out of memories he imagined new and even more painful injuries with which to torment his brother. Ronny got smart and came to bed with squares of toilet paper, which he then spit on and made into earplugs. He listened to his brother's muffled words for a few minutes but then he took one earplug out. When he had got the gist of the injury he put the plug back in, but a few minutes later he started worrying, and he took the plug out again. In and out, in and out until finally Ian fell asleep and there was only the sound of their father's low voice coming from the far-off kitchen, where he often sat up badgering their mother about her poor handling of family accounts.

When he was eleven, Ian got cancer and two years later had to have his leg amputated. He came out of the anaesthesia crying, really screaming, and for weeks and months he said his leg was killing him. His father said it would go away. Everyone was always saying the wrong thing; everyone's hands were always to their mouths. Ronny did not need to put toilet paper in his ears any more, but he found that the only way he could get to sleep was to dredge up one of Ian's old hockey injuries.

According to Belgian custom, single girls turned into old maids when they were twenty-five. At twelve, Lise had a few years to go, but there were signs, and her mother worried about it. What was the harm, her mother asked, in allowing her older brother to be right now and then? But he wasn't right, Lise said. Why should she say he was right just because he was in the polytechnic? And don't worry, she told her mother, she wasn't going to marry *him*.

Now there was a space between an old man and two business women. But the old man was walking so slowly that Lise was sure the women would catch up. She put her head out into the drizzle and got her spit ready and let it go the instant the old man's head was out of the way.

Ian hated getting special permission to get out of classes a few minutes early. He hated being alone, pegging himself down the long school halls, his leg hurting like hell. Thirteen fucking years old and his goddamn leg. Jesus fucking Christ. His marks went down and he lost his colour and his friends had to tell the caseworker they guessed Ian could be into drugs; they had not seen much of him since, well, since he lost his leg.

As usual, Lise's father had left the window open, so she could hear some of the things he said to the girl. He said the same sorts of things to all of them, a fact that was both horrible and comforting to Lise. Her father was short, almost a dwarf, and he liked tall, fat girls. He told them to undress, and as soon as they got started he told them they were growing fat. "Don't you care if the young men laugh at you and call you fatso? I suppose you think I enjoy examining your type. I suppose you think it gives me pleasure to touch you here. As I must. It hurts? It doesn't hurt. And there's no use spreading your legs like that. You can't imagine I find you attractive." Of course he had never seen them before. And no girl would come back a second time. One time he examined a girl for three hours. He told her that her womb was badly placed. "But you aren't the motherly type," he added. "Your type never is."

Lise saw the girl leave the building and go weaving in great w's down the street to avoid touching other people. The girl turned abruptly, and practically fell into the Stella Bar at the corner, and Lise, surprised at her own reaction, flew down the five flights of stairs after her, nearly losing one shoe because she had not properly pulled it on. She was thinking, Jerk, bastard, prick! Putting her father in a list, like the lists they made at school: "Join the word with its correct meaning." Bastard! Prick! Jerk! She drew a line from each word to her father.

The girl was not in the Stella Bar after all, and it was full of men, full of fathers. Lise walked on to the Grande Place. There was a girl sitting by the fountain, but it wasn't the same girl. Lise spit into the fountain and then blessed the spit in the name of the Father, the Son and the Holy Ghost. She had been spitting a lot lately; there was always something stuck in her throat. She had had bronchitis twice since she turned twelve. The first time there were complications and she got pneumonia and her mother talked about having the priest come in, but her father would not allow it. That was when Lise started blessing her spit. She was going to manage without a blessing from God, the father of fathers.

The following day in school she was drawing the negative space around the chair of the classmate in front of her when it came to her that she would marry no man. Instead she would have affairs with men like Monsieur Langevin, her drawing instructor. Monsieur Langevin was not like her father or any father. He was from France and he talked slowly, as if he did not expect them to understand much because they were Belgian. He said,

Oh, you Belgians, with real sympathy. And he was passionate about negative space. He illustrated it with a slide of the Eiffel Tower and Marie-Cécile giggled because the slide was upside down. Marie-Cécile giggled at everything because she had bad nerves. Lise often felt the urge to spit and bless her spit when she thought of Marie-Cécile. She wanted to protect herself from what could be catching. Marie-Cécile had no eyelashes and everything about her was thin, even her hair. Lise's father would never examine such a girl.

Lise was thinking about Marie-Cécile when it came to her that negative space was everywhere where her father was not. She decided that the negative space around the Eiffel Tower was as important, no, more important than the Eiffel Tower itself.

When she was twenty-five Lise's brother asked her if she was still going to go to the Grande Place on Saint Catherine's Day, and Lise said why not? and went with her friends. That was where she met Ian, who was pegging around the square with a tripod. The point of the celebration, she explained to Ian, was to round up and laugh at all the old maids. And this year she was one of them.

Was it something to be proud of, then? Ian asked. Lise said of course it wasn't. Did Canadian girls like to be old maids? She knew better than to take Ian for an American, even though she could not tell the difference. The difference was that if it turned out he was Canadian he would take offense.

Lise went with Ian to see the photographs he had taken of Brussels. He walked faster than she was used to walking and had no trouble getting up the four flights of stairs to his hotel room. When she looked out of his window and saw the old maids passing in the street, weaving and staggering, some of them, from the beer they had bought each other as consolation for their lot, Lise had a sudden urge to be kissed. She told Ian that there was something in the street that they would see better if the room was dark, and when he had switched out the lights she took his hand and put it around her waist, under her blouse, and held it under her own against her damp skin. She drew close, and he kissed her neck. Then she realized she did not want him to kiss her after all, but only to talk to her and touch her while he talked.

She lay back on the bed on her elbows and spread her legs, and pulled him to her side. The instant he stopped talking and tried to climb up beside her she shook him off. "Don't glue your lips to me like a leech, silly," she said. And she told him to please keep talking because the darkness made her feel afraid, and especially, she lied, on Saint Catherine's Day.

Ian laughed and said she was a funny, funny girl, not like any Canadian he had ever met.

They fell in love that night, and even though Lise knew it could have been someone different, she followed Ian to his enormous Canada. Since she never wanted to make love, Ian assumed that she wanted to be married, and so he asked her to, in a short, generous speech. Lise told Ian she had long ago decided to marry no man, but to have affairs.

But we're not even having a goddamn affair, Ian shouted. They both knew he was shouting about his leg, and Lise felt sorry for him and convinced him to stay with her for another month like that, not making love. Ian learned to fit in mean things as he talked to her and stroked her. "Your thighs are getting fleshy," he said. "Do you think I like having to see them and touch them this way?"

One day Ian told Lise that if she would not make love like other girls then he wanted out, and Lise said that was fine, she was tired of Canada anyway. She flew back to Belgium and called her old drawing teacher. Monsieur Langevin had never agreed to have an affair with her, but he had said he would always be at her disposal if she needed help of any kind. As usual, he asked sympathetic questions. Lise told him that she felt no different. Why should she? She and her ex-boyfriend had only done away with the thing between them, which was mostly in their heads anyway. All it meant was that she had to go back to imagining Monsieur Langevin at night. "Yes, you," she laughed. Monsieur Langevin cleared his throat. He said she was going through an unfortunate and undoubtedly difficult period.

At first Lise went to her parents' for dinner once a week, and when she lost her job because of her poor attitude, it was a simple thing to move back into her little room on the fourth floor. She sat for hours at the open window, closing her eyes as the drizzle blew gently across her face.

There were no more chubby girls leaving the building because her father had sold his practice and retired, but Lise kept watching, and then one afternoon there was a chubby girl. Lise watched the girl struggle to open her umbrella and veer sharply away from the people queuing up for the tram, and as she watched Lise felt a strong pain, something like a menstrual cramp, begin to take form deep in her belly. She pulled the telephone directory out from under her bed and then had trouble deciding whether to look up an analyst or a gynaecologist. She had rehearsed this moment, read through the names so many times that the pages listing analysts and gynaecologists were curled.

A came before G, but she knew her pain was real. Her blouse was damp and clinging, and she thought, as she dialled the number of the gynaecologist she knew had bought her father's practice, that she would be well-advised to run a quick bath. She mixed up the last two numbers, and had to dial again. This made her laugh, and she thought of Marie-Cécile, and then she needed to spit. She pulled the telephone as far to the window as the cord allowed, and when she still couldn't reach, she considered hanging up, or leaving the receiver to dangle. But at that moment the receptionist answered. Lise excused herself, and spit into her free hand, and waved her other hand, the one holding the receiver, through the air to bless the spit. She began to laugh again and wanted badly to stop, because she knew that if she kept laughing the receptionist would never believe she had a pain.

THE WEEPERS

In the martial arts it is good to keep half your breath. As you kick, you give a sharp, low yell, using your diaphragm, and you cut the breath off on its way out. The half-breath you've saved will be useful if your opponent gets you in a stranglehold.

But no one needs to take half a breath with them when they die. The first woman in history, Queen Hatshepsut, who gave King Thutmose III a hard time in the Eighteenth Egyptian Dynasty, might have tried to take half a breath along with her when she died. It was probably Thutmose's intention, when he had her face scratched out of the mural in his tomb, to reach into the hereafter and strangle her.

But the days of loading up graves were over in most parts of the world when Adrian began to die. The dying were taken to hospitals and given green gowns. These were not burial gowns, and it wouldn't occur to a dying patient to ask to keep one. Rubies and favourite cats are one thing, but no one is going to make much of an effort to hang on to a cotton gown the colour of infection, a colour that makes clean toenails look grey.

Adrian lived alone. His parents had been dead several years, and he'd lost all his friends through neglect and malice. He rented a basement room in a stucco bungalow with pinkish trim, half a block north of Hastings Street on Springer Avenue.

It was a dull block: there were no plastic flamingos, no portal lions, no woodchip lawns. No one bothered to cross rose strains or to use edgers. When the chestnut branches grazed the power line, Adrian's neighbour (whose name he didn't know) hauled a coil of thick orange cord over the lawn, propped a chain-saw against his hip, and joylessly felled the whole tree. He then spent the afternoon sawing it into firewood rounds. The sawdust clotted among the fallen leaves until all turned brown and Mrs. Genezi, Adrian's landlady, came out in rubber boots and gardening gloves and her husband's windbreaker to rake the mess up. She raked well onto the neighbour's side and filled three big garbage bags.

Adrian, returning from the 7-Eleven, where he'd gone for milk, wondered briefly, as he leaned to keep his balance on the hill up from Hastings Street, about the neighbourhood children. They might miss playing in the chestnut tree. On the other hand, they might prefer playing on the new stump: they could jump from it into the leaves, although certainly the now-soggy leaves would have lost some of their appeal. And as Mrs. Genezi looked up from the third twist-tie, Adrian saw the thoroughly raked lawn, and he told himself that after all there weren't many children in the neighbourhood, and not once had he seen any playing in or around the chestnut tree. He insisted on carrying the bags out to the alley.

A few days later he lay on what had suddenly become his deathbed, with his first weeper, Marsha, in attendance, and as he stared at the ceiling it came to him that this sappy thinking about the children and their jumping games had been a warning sign that he was very ill. But hardly sappy enough, he felt, to justify the overnight transformations. One day his face had been an indivisible live sculpture, rough skin blemished with ingrown whiskers over the throat, and the next, a clumsy Saran Wrap of reptilian hue lumping together flesh and bones as slippery and disconnected as packaged chicken legs. The skin was drawn over the nose bridge and cheekbones, and yet it overlapped, sagging, under the eyes and ears. His lumpy mattress and fifteen-year-old box-spring were now a damp, rancid deathbed. All this before the municipality had collected Mrs. Genezi's three garbage bags.

In the eighteenth century people began to fear death, and it became unfashionable — unthinkable — to keep the dying at home. Hospitals sprang up all over the world. By the second half of the twentieth century, people couldn't even talk about death. They certainly didn't wait for the dying to smell before they put them in the hospital, and there the beds were on rollers; when a patient's rate of dying accelerated sharply, he was wheeled to another ward.

"But what luck," Mrs. Genezi told her friend Pia over the telephone. "The poor man dying at the beginning of a hospital strike."

"Did you dial 999?" Pia worked at the edges of the sticker on her telephone that read, "IN CASE OF DYING, DIAL 999." Presumably, the caller would reach a volunteer trained to gather people who would help. A trick to enhance privatization, Pia thought, but now, with the strike, a welcome resource for her friend, who had once been so helpful in the Department of Romance Languages, where Pia had come close to taking a degree in Italian.

But Alura Genezi would not have her house full of professionals or volunteers. She waited for Adrian's friends and family to take him home with them. But no one called or came, and this, she said, was when she'd remembered her Italian grandmother and the custom of weepers.

Pia was all for it. Never mind the good that weepers would do Adrian, drawing out his memories, helping him through his last door, encouraging him to leave every bit of breath on this side. "It will help you, Alura," Pia said. "And if it works! We'll have a new social model!" Pia was presently concerned with sociopolitical history and saw the weepers idea as a sort of division of labour.

"In my grandmother's village, everybody knew everybody else," Mrs. Genezi said. "And the really good weepers were known across the country." But how did one find a good weeper in Adrian's twentieth-century Burnaby?

"Get his address book," Pia said. "Call the names with lots of crossed-out numbers."

Mrs. Genezi sat in her sunny kitchen nook with the telephone and the pantyhose liner Adrian had propped above his extension. The liner was ruled in red ballpoint, rather more evenly at the top. The last spaces were empty. The only doodles were the enlarged dots which followed some of the numbers. Two men's names were listed, and neither was home.

The women were disappointing.

The first one Mrs. Genezi found home said, "Oh, he won't want to see me. He hates me."

"Adrian? Adrian owes me five hundred dollars," said the second. "You tell him that, see if he wants to see me."

"I only arranged his vacation. . . .We went out once or twice . . . " said another.

And the last one made a racket — washing the dishes, Mrs. Genezi supposed — so she had to ask everything twice. "I've never heard of him," this one said. "We just moved."

Pia told Mrs. Genezi not to give up. "Call them back, ask if they know anyone else who might know him," she said.

This time Mrs. Genezi got some leads. "Yes . . . some dancer. Nicole," said one. "Oh, yes: Nicole Lapointe. A French girl."

"I can't imagine him having a girlfriend," said another. "I mean I practically had to . . . sometimes I wondered if he was gay or what. He talked about a woman called Hannah, but who knows. Hannah Lind."

Then there was the woman washing dishes. "Didn't you just call? Honestly, I don't know him. Wait, there's a name on the wall, 'Marsha,' do you want the number?"

Within the hour, Mrs. Genezi had lined up three old girlfriends for that evening. "You don't think we're rushing things?" she asked.

"Why wait until he's dead?" And Pia, who had no family commitments of her own, offered to come over around eight o'clock.

At eight-fifteen she stood by the chair at Adrian's bedside — a funny old chair that made her think of the ones Van Gogh had first drawn — and was thinking of priests and surgeons when a woman with dark-stockinged legs clicked by the squat window. Adrian, who had not looked anywhere but at the ceiling, seemed to stiffen at the polite knocking.

Mrs. Genezi looked at her husband's watch, which, since the leather strap had disintegrated, she now wore on a chain. "That will be Marsha. She asked could she weep between nine and ten o'clock this evening; she had a party to go to, or perhaps it was mass."

Marsha was thin and breathless. She held her dripping umbrella out as if it were a divining rod, and Mrs. Genezi stood it firmly against the wall and brought Marsha downstairs to Adrian's bedside. "Pia's here," she said. "But you asked to go first. I haven't forgotten."

Marsha held back as if Adrian were a wounded scavenger.

"Is he. . . how is he?"

Mrs. Genezi ignored this. "Please, just begin — we're here if you need us, but go ahead as if we weren't." She set two more Van Gogh chairs by the window.

Marsha gripped the chair.

"Adrian? I hope you're not feeling too, too . . . "

"Don't worry about how he's feeling, dear, just start remembering the life you shared," Mrs. Genezi said. There was a loud knocking at the basement entrance. Mrs. Genezi waved at Marsha to go ahead and went silently, briskly, to the door. Never, thought Pia, had she seen her widowed friend so completely at ease.

"I'm Nicole," said the visitor. "The second weeper? I figured he'd live in a basement."

"Good, come in, Nicole. You're so kind to come, and Marsha has started us off — if you wouldn't mind waiting — let me take your coat." Mrs. Genezi took Nicole's fur and led her smoothly to a chair.

"Adrian?" Marsha was saying. "I . . . it's too bad it had to wait until you . . . we've just let our lives go on . . . I suppose I couldn't . . . "

"The memories, dear," Mrs. Genezi said. "Coffee?" she mouthed to Pia and Nicole. She waved Pia to stay sitting down, and the three of them turned back to Marsha and Adrian.

Marsha sighed. "Adrian, we did have some good times. Some very good times. Do you remember?"

Adrian blinked.

"For instance," Marsha began again, raising her fingers, "For instance walking in the leaves, yes — when we lived in Montreal, we used to walk on the mountain, do you remember the squirrels, we always stopped to watch the squirrels . . . "

Nicole groaned and moved up to the window alcove. Marsha glanced around. "And on the beach," she continued. "That was here in Vancouver of course, the sound of the waves . . . and the halo the moon got." Marsha sounded panicky. "And then walking down the streets at night, oh, on Robson Street, or St. Catherine's . . . and then there was walking around the seawall in Stanley Park . . . "

"Enough walking, Christ. What about fucking?" Nicole was swinging her high-booted legs.

"Oh, I always enjoyed making love with him. With you, Adrian," Marsha said quickly, nodding. "Sex was very good. There was no problem with sex. No, sex was fine. It was very good." She leaned forward, toyed with the sheet, then dropped it with a movement of self-consciousness. Adrian stared at the ceiling. "Oh, there were good times . . . some very good times . . . I . . . I hope I've helped in some small way . . . "

"Gag," Nicole said.

Marsha turned to Mrs. Genezi. "Is this what you were looking for?"

"Me? I'm not looking. I'm not dying. But you're finished? Thank you very much, Marsha. No, please stay, I've got cake."

She showed Marsha to the chair beside Pia and motioned Nicole to go next. Marsha looked miserable.

Nicole walked stiffly to the bedside. She stared down at the dying man's face.

The doorbell rang, and Mrs. Genezi got up again.

"I don't know, Ade," Nicole said. "Hard to pack it into a few minutes." She called up at Mrs. Genezi, who was showing a red-cheeked woman down the stairs. "How long have I got?"

Mrs. Genezi shrugged. "Take as long as you need. This is Hannah, the third weeper. Pia, Marsha and Nicole. So you're all here. I'll get the coffee," she said. She motioned Marsha to stay put in her chair. "They might need you," she said. When she came back she pulled her chair nearer to the radiator and settled in. Marsha was gripping her chair again; Pia was taking notes.

"Might as well start with money," Nicole said. "No way I was going to ask my uncle in Versailles again, and you said, 'Well, then, chérie, why don't you just jump on a hovercraft?' — and you took that antique chair — well, everything in the castle was antique — and threw it into the mirror? But we made up that time, remember? God, it was cold in that place, and old Jean-Jacques several hundred rooms away . . . God, we had nothing else to do but fight and fuck . . . "

For a moment Nicole's expression was affectionate.

"Which reminds me of your jealousy," she said. "Remember you used to ask why I wanted to see my friends? You didn't say, 'Don't go,' or 'I want to have you all to myself.' You said, really slimy, 'So, Nicole, why do you think you have to hang around with that Betsy Ringer?' You said she was going to end up in an asylum. Just because you couldn't stand how you'd walk in and there we'd be at the table. We'd be drinking coffee, and Betsy'd have an ashtray full of butts and she wouldn't even look up.

"You said I had tendencies myself. Me, neurotic! You just wanted to know what I was thinking. At all times. Where I was going and who with. 'Why don'tcha come, Adie?' I'd say. 'Because I don't find those people very interesting,' you'd say. I didn't find you very interesting, either." Nicole looked around at the others, who were breathing in and out in a sleepy way. "I'm getting to sex," she said. She turned back to Adrian and sat down.

"Sex," she said. She said it again, slowly: "Sex. Making love. Did we have any idea what that meant?"

"He's looking!" cried Marsha. The three women jumped up. Marsha was right: Adrian had turned his head, ever so slightly, towards Nicole.

"This is very good," said Mrs. Genezi.

"Sex. Making love. Sex," Nicole said quickly. "That's what you want to hear about, is it?" She laughed. "Well, you know . . . it was all right, Ade. Sometimes you let go. Remember we were camping, and we nearly started a forest fire, we had to haul water from the lake in jerry cans, and we were running around, coughing, so scared, then when we got that under control, we came together, accidentally, and we started fucking on the ashes, everything was wet and steaming, it was like the dawn of time, and we kept going and going, remember?"

Adrian nodded slightly.

"Yeah, well, that was the only really good time," Nicole said. She sniffed, looking him right in the eyes. "And all those women where you worked, and then you on about the men I saw. Who? Harold? You know, the funny thing is I did try to go out with Harold after. Did you know that? He was even more of a controller than you. Well, Ade. I think I'll give this a rest." Nicole got up. She leaned over and squeezed Adrian's hand, which lay grey over the white sheet. Adrian didn't squeeze back. "Go for it," she said, turning, waving her braceleted hand at Hannah.

But it was Marsha who got up. "I . . . remembered something," she said.

"Of course, dear," Mrs. Genezi said.

"Adrian?" Marsha stood beside the deathbed. She clenched

and unclenched her hand. Adrian had gone back to looking at the ceiling.

"Adrian, I . . . "

"What are you afraid of, Marsha? Losing him?" Nicole laughed. "He's dying."

"I know that." Marsha's voice was lower, stronger, now. "Adrian? There are some things we both need to remember. I didn't say them before, because I thought . . . "

"Why not cut the intro," Nicole said.

Marsha whirled around. "Why not shut up!"

Nicole might have been looking with her tongue for some gum in her mouth. She shrugged, looked down from her alcove spot to Mrs. Genezi and Hannah and Pia.

"Go ahead, dear," Mrs. Genezi said.

"Okay. Okay, Adrian. It's hard to imagine you, sick like this, grey . . . you look very bad. It's hard to imagine you once kicked me around. I think, I try to think, what did I do to deserve that? You didn't drink. And I always knew when it was coming. But I never knew why."

Adrian stared at the ceiling.

"Isn't that something," Nicole said flatly. "He beat you and he doesn't remember. Beat you and you don't know why! He never beat me, I'll tell you."

"Maybe he never loved you, either," Marsha said. She put her hand over her mouth.

"Oh, love! Love and sex and death! That's what sells products. God, it's women like you . . . " Nicole trailed off. She started swinging her leg again.

"You do remember, don't you, Adrian?" Marsha said. But Adrian was looking at the ceiling.

"Help him remember," Mrs. Genezi said gently.

"Okay: we'd been to a movie and you saw a car for sale and you got upset because I didn't like the colour."

"Holy Christ," Nicole said.

"You wanted to walk by it again, but I was in heels, it was freezing . . . I wasn't enthusiastic . . . so when we were at the owner's house you were polite to him so I knew you were upset, and I was scared. All the way home I was asking you things, thinking, I won't talk about the car, that will upset him, no, that's not right, I will talk about the car, because that's why he's upset, he thinks I don't like the colour, but then he'll know I'm just lying if I say I like it now, unless I can convince him I've changed my mind? You know? Remember?"

Adrian was still staring at the ceiling.

"So we got in the door and you just kicked off your shoes and went into the living room and sat down on the couch and turned on the television. I came in and asked what you were watching, and bam! You just smacked me across the face, asked me how I thought I could get off with the way I was acting, and I asked you which way, and you said, 'Oh, Christ, don't play this game with me,' and you hit me again. Remember? Don't you remember?"

"This is very good," Mrs. Genezi said. She took Pia's hand and held it on her flowered lap. Nicole stopped swinging her legs. And still Adrian stared at the ceiling.

"Go to hell, then," Marsha said. She took a Kleenex from the box Mrs. Genezi handed her, but she didn't use it; she wasn't crying. "You go ahead," she said angrily to Hannah, not looking at her.

Hannah had the flush of women who are well-loved. "It's me, Adrian," she said. "Hannah Lind. I don't think I'm angry with you. It was a long time ago. Our big deal was when I got pregnant. You said you were sorry, but you were too young . . . you just couldn't take the responsibility . . . you had a lot of travelling to do . . . you were even crying. I walked out. I hoped you'd come after me but you didn't. I took the train. I kept thinking, I'm pregnant, and I'm taking a train by myself. I was only scared of the idea. But I had a miscarriage.

"What else. Oh: remember a couple years later you showed up with your camera? That struck me because we never took pictures of each other when we were lovers. And then when we ran into each other in the airport. You were fat, smoking a lot." Hannah laughed. "If it had been ten years earlier and me fat and smoking, you would have said, 'Put on a little weight?' But I couldn't say it."

"So say it now." Nicole offered the others sticks of gum. Pia saw that it wasn't sugarless, and mouthed, 'No thanks.' Nicole flicked the wrapper into the wastebasket and made snapping noises.

Hannah shrugged. "We had about twenty minutes before our planes left, and it was hard to think of things to say. I realized you were never very interesting. You were just blond, sort of good-looking. When you were young.

"And that time you talked me into coming over to that room on, what was it, Burnaby Street? I think you wanted money but I can't remember: the place smelled terrible, and your eyes were so dull . . . that was five years ago? So you were forty? You looked wasted. You look a lot better now even though you're . . . you know what I mean. And you said I looked good and I knew it. I guess I was the ugly duckling." Hannah was forty and looked thirty. "It's hard to believe he's going to die," she said, turning to Mrs. Genezi. "I keep thinking I should look at him in a different way. Are you really going to die, Adrian?" she asked gently. Adrian stared at the ceiling, but made a tentative, reaching gesture with his hand. A purple starfish. "Yes, you are," she said softly. "You must have a lot of regrets."

Pia squeezed Mrs. Genezi's hand. "What a terrible life!" she whispered.

Mrs. Genezi nodded. "You try," she said. "Try going further back."

Then Adrian spoke.

"I'm only one man," he said to the ceiling.

"Of course," Pia said easily, settling into the deathbed chair. "You're Adrian."

"Please . . . " Adrian's eyes closed.

"Don't worry, Adrian," Pia said briskly. "Ade. Adie. Do you remember when we were in kindergarten? We used to hang on the monkeybars, you at your end, and me at my end — in my kilt. You had a funny smile upside down. Sometimes I held my skirt so it wouldn't go over my head, and sometimes I didn't.

"Remember your mother made cake with cinnamon and apples? And on the first day of school you told the teacher you had to go straight home because your mother was waiting with cake? I asked my mother if I could go to your house after school, and then I asked you if I could come to your house after school . . . " Pia gave a happy little sigh.

"Kindergarten! Then you moved away . . . I didn't know you were moving until you had gone, and then I didn't believe it. But then we moved! I was sitting at the front of the second row in my new school, and I turned around and there you were in your same spot! We traced leaves and you let me use your jackknife to whittle. In grade three we practised kissing. I told Cindy and Mayda I knew a boy we could kiss. Remember them? The twins? Remember how I warned you first in a note so you could keep your mouth closed?"

Now Adrian was smiling. Hannah and Marsha raised their eyebrows; Nicole snapped her gum; Mrs. Genezi nodded gently.

"When did we go on that overnight field trip? Were we already in junior high? It was so cold, and someone said we should zip our bags together and roll up in a big line. You and I were swearing; you said it was neat that I was a girl and I could swear. . . . We went skiing; we graduated, we couldn't stop making love, and if it wasn't safe or whatever and we couldn't make love, you put your hand just there and I came and came. Oh, Adrian."

Adrian was blinking. He started to sniff, and his chest rose and fell in jerks. He was having trouble getting the air out.

"You went to university back east but the second year we couldn't stand it and I moved east too . . . we lived in a two- and-a-half and there were all those bugs . . . we ate spaghetti all the time with no meat in it at all. . . . Remember, Adie? Then we got married, and we both worked for a few years, and then we had our first baby. . . . She was perfect. . . . She hasn't had an easy life, but she's doing well, she married a lawyer in Toronto . . . and our son has just started pre-med at McGill. . . . You always say to me, 'Pia . . . we are so happy.' Do you remember?"

Adrian nodded. "I remember," he said. The tears were running down his cheeks.

"We've done everything, Ade," Pia said.

"Everything," Adrian said. "I am dying, and we have been happy." And with his eyes still shut, he groped for Pia's hand, and his breathing slowed.

RULES FOR THE LIVING

Arlene waited for the girl to take back her pen. She was wondering what the girl was writing — something about the boy beside her on the log? — when she saw her Nana at the bottom of Davie Street. Nana was dead and had been dead for years, but there she was, good as new in an odd-looking green dress. A tent-dress, they used to call them. The light changed, and Nana led the way across Denman Street. In one hand she carried a shopping bag, in the other, a book.

She stood a moment at the traffic triangle looking out at the freighters, knee-deep, from where Arlene sat, in a pool of red and blue flowers. Then — and Arlene could hear this from memory — she shook down her armload of silver bracelets, crossed Beach Avenue, and continued along the footpath to the beach. She might have arrived on a tour bus to visit royalty; she might herself have been royalty. Arlene was too delighted by her dead grandmother's appearance to doubt it.

The girl got her pen back and bent over her notebook. She was thinking of a type of church where the women were supposed to wear their hair long. She herself had long, dark hair, but it was the fly-away kind, and although it reached her bra in the back, people didn't think of her hair at all. Girls her age saw her as that-poor-girl-with-no-eyelashes, and women thought of her as someone vulnerable to ads for skin creams, a girl who tried to cover up by carrying around that notebook. She held it firmly now, tilted up from her bare knees like a sketchbook, but she was writing with such concentration that Arlene did not feel pity but a kind of excitement, the urgency of a spy. For entire moments she held her breath, and her world collapsed into one wish: she wanted to know what the girl was writing.

She would not have guessed the boy had anything to do with her until he reached over and seized her pen. Then he crossed one of his legs over her white ankles — you could say he pinned them in place in the sand. He drank from a paper cup, and his smooth shoulders touched hers each time he lifted it. He was a simple-looking boy with a lot of red hair. Arlene imagined him pacified for the next five years with his music, with Big-Gulps, beer, a succession of cars and action movies, and a girl to talk babytalk with when he was in the mood. The girl kicked off his leg and continued writing.

"If you are Christian, do not cut your hair," the girl wrote. Her name was Cindy, but she wished it were less common and was continually trying out new ones. She bought a baby-name book at Coles, and she read through it, looking up the girls from school, wondering who got the names Amanda, Amy, Annette and Ardelle. Zelda. She thought about foreign girls who had accents.

She sighed. Bernard — Beanie — was not her boyfriend. They had broken up and were now friends. She watched him drinking, studied the parts of his throat and chest working together as he swallowed, observed the muscles in his arms and neck soften as he resumed his ordinary sitting position. He was a machine. Or a cancer patient; but that would make her the nurse. She crossed out "Do not cut your hair" and wrote "Try to grow your hair long."

She was squinting because she had no sunglasses. Beanie had, but his didn't block out all the rays. They fooled the eyes; they were worse than nothing. "Don't wear cheap sunglasses," she wrote. "Look for ones that block out UVAs and UVBs. Don't," she wrote, starting a new page, "start going out with a boy who calls himself Beanie. Heed your first impulse, and flee." If she had been at home in her room, she would have ripped this page out and turned on the radio to see if there were any good songs on. As it was, she didn't wish to attract attention. "Don't try to make things perfect," she wrote, and added, "Seek perfection, but don't demand it."

Nana was close enough now that Arlene could read the title of her paperback: *12 Stories by Chekhov*. "Nana?" Arlene raised her voice. "Nana?"

Her grandmother had never worn green and had read little apart from the *Christian Science Monitor*. When she understood that Arlene was speaking to her, she frowned, and her long face came in front of the sun. Arlene remembered her as laughing, but not frowning. Pursed lips, yes, and a slight frown the time Arlene told her straight out she did not want to train to become a lawyer's secretary. But a very short frown, and then more tea, another cookie, a tube of hand cream to take back to her student apartment. And Arlene remembered her hair as silver, but here it was yellowish, matted like the fur of an old stuffed animal.

"'Nana?'" the old woman said. "Are you related? To Agnes? Mrs. P. William Black?

Arlene nodded but the woman went straight on. "That's one hundred percent cotton, isn't it?" She pointed to Arlene's sundress. "We still get a lot of Permapress. Easy Care. It's what old people come with. Though Kevin had two Permapress shirts for the office. I hung them over the bath."

"Kevin?" Arlene's grandfather was Paul; at the bank he was William.

Now the old woman had her elbows raised like a seagull. She eyed the grass around her. "Are there ants?" she said. "I'm phobic." She clung to her sunglasses and sat down.

12 Stories by Chekhov. Nana would never read Russian literature. *Doctor Zhivago*, possibly. And yet, there was the smell of rose water; there were the bracelets jangling as the old woman smoothed her hair. Arlene shook her head, let her eyes fill with tears.

Bernard made his eyes follow the instructor at the wind-surfing place, but it was a strain. The way she led her students in stretching exercises, you could tell she knew she had a good build. For fun Bernard swung around and read out loud from Cindy's diary. "'I'm not his girlfriend — '" he began in a high voice, "'we're just friends. I'm not his girlfriend — we're just . . . '" but then Cindy snapped it shut. Was she filling the whole book with that? Bernard looked away, pleased.

She wasn't. It was a trick to avoid writer's block. "Keep repeating the last sentence you wrote until a new one comes," the writing magazine suggested. And a new sentence did come. "Don't be hurt by humans when they disappoint you," she wrote. "Don't try to change them to be who you want." The next time she looked up Beanie was back looking at the surfers. And oh, even better, here comes fat old Michael with some music, and I wonder what he's got in the duffle bag.

Arlene offered sunscreen to the woman who looked like but could not be Nana. "Number 29," she said.

The woman said it smelled like Avon. She sold Avon when they were in Rupert. She smoothed the cream over her arm, and the skin hung from her elbow the way Nana's had. Arlene began to feel angry. "My grandmother never lived in B.C.," she said. "Desperate people going further and further west until they fell in the ocean. She'd rather starve. But you *look* like her."

"It's the body." The woman smoothed the hem of the dress Nana wouldn't have put on to do the vacuuming. "I was Teresa Blackstone," she said. "I hardly know Mrs. P.W. I came down for the SeaFest. The fireworks. I used to love them." She smiled, as if this cleared up everything, and once again she was Nana, her teeth so large that her jaw curved out just to hold them.

"Don't do things to please others," the dark-haired girl wrote. "Not unless you won't be hurt when they forget you, or unless," she added, "unless they have a terminal illness." There were always exceptions. Possibly the exceptions should have a column to themselves.

Michael and Beanie held the paper cup under the sports bag. They were giving it a transfusion. "Don't think you really know anyone, even if you have slept with them," the girl wrote. "Even — " and she changed this to "especially." "Especially if you were a virgin before." Thank God she hadn't slept with Beanie. "Don't depend on your own advice; neither should you ignore it when it's good."

Teresa Blackstone. That could be a Catholic name. Nana was, she said, a "Protestant from the North." Did Nana know there was a Catholic woman in her body? Was the tent-dress Nana's?

The woman said she must be kidding. She opened the shopping bag and showed Arlene a powder blue dress. "Polyester crêpe? Even your grandmother's tired of it. She wasn't my first choice, you know. But she was free." Teresa Blackstone had bought the dress up the street. "At Gazeby." She had seen the leggings Arlene was wearing and liked them, but she thought they were lingerie. "With this body?" she said. "That would be criminal."

"Gazebo," Arlene said. These days, she explained, you could wear a brassiere down the street if you liked.

Arlene tried to think of something important to talk about, to ask the woman. About her Nana, about the afterworld. She was having trouble not speculating on what it must mean, in the afterworld, to be considered free.

"Up there," Teresa was saying, "you have to wait until someone dies." You watched, you waited, you exchanged. It was the only way to get a new outfit — or a different body. "I couldn't have come down in my own body," she said. "I died in a crash — I've got no legs. I'm paralysed up there in the same thing I had on, my leathers and my red pumps. Doesn't matter how sick of them I get. Come-fuck-me pumps, we used to call them. And no underwear at all." She laughed. "Don't worry. Your grandmother isn't wearing the leathers. I had a T-shirt in my bag, for sleeping."

She showed Arlene her new sunglasses. "They were on sale at the cash. Two ninety-nine."

They might screen out flies, Arlene thought. But what did cancer matter if you were already dead?

Vancouver was big, the woman remarked. The beach was crowded.

Arlene could only nod. She spotted a couple from her high-rise on a bench, and, cross-legged in front of them, a heavy man was singing "Sounds of Silence." He had bandaged the blue velour of his guitar case with packing tape; some of it was unstuck and flitting in the breeze. Two men in stretch shorts strolled by. One made such wide gestures that a runner had to detour around them through the sand. The runner's breath was rasping.

There was no end to pain, Arlene reflected. She did not like to think about old people. Nana was tired of powder blue. Even in heaven you got tired. What a set-up. "*That* colour does nothing for her skin tone," she remarked spitefully.

The woman who claimed to be Teresa Blackstone shrugged and said, "I can't help it, she was *old*."

Arlene realized what this had to mean.

"How old did you think I was? I was like *her*," Teresa said.

She pointed to the dark-haired girl who was still writing, but also taking drinks from the fat boy's beer each time he dug it into the sand to fiddle with his tape player.

Dead? That girl? Arlene did not hear the woman ask about fast food. Something about fries and when the fireworks were going to start, and where would be a good place to watch.

"Watch what?"

"From up there you just see smoke," Teresa was saying. "I hope it's better from the ground," she said suddenly, "or why bother coming back?"

Two roller-bladers veered around an elderly couple who had drifted into the cycle lane, and this pushed Arlene onto Teresa's lap. "Fun," Teresa said. "Kevin used to skateboard. And there *they* go." It was the three teenagers. The girl with the notebook led. She continued to write as she walked. The fat boy carried his tape player; the music might have been a rap version of a Catholic mass. "She should cut that hair," Teresa remarked. "It's so thin."

Without speaking, Arlene and Teresa got up and followed the teenagers. The girl was writing, "Don't judge a person by the company they keep. And don't judge the company by the way they look. They could look like garbage pickers and be extremely intelligent." Arlene strained to read it, and the girl walked faster. Arlene took Teresa's arm to hurry her along. "Would you like to do some more shopping?" she asked. "The fireworks don't start until ten."

But the girl stopped at the first coffee place. She settled herself at an outside table and resumed writing. The fat boy put his tape player at her feet, told her to watch it, and followed red-haired Bernard inside.

Teresa Blackstone had also stopped. "Cappuccino," she breathed. "We don't get that yet. Would you mind?"

There was a table next to the girl's; Arlene had her hand on the chair. She picked up a flyer. "'Creative Visualization. Breaking the barriers of time and space.' I tried that," she said. She was going to ask if they had Creative Visualization up there, but Teresa was staring at a garbage picker.

Something about him, the way his hip-hugger jeans were back in fashion — for young people, at least — or the way he poked around, his face reddened by drink and optimism, something made Arlene reflect that she was living through an extraordinary occurrence. She must ask questions about the afterlife! Solve family mysteries! She began by asking Teresa if she knew her grandfather.

"Not personally." Teresa did know he died years before Mrs. P.W. The garbage picker moved on, and Teresa played with the foam on her coffee. She was easily distracted. You had to think quickly.

"But you knew he was my grandmother's husband?" Arlene said.

Teresa wasn't listening. "See that girl? See her outfit?" She pointed. "I had one like it. I looked cool."

"Ah. And you've met my grandfather? You knew they were related?"

"Sure." Teresa was vague. "I think he's with someone else now. *Oh God*, that's the bike we smashed up on. Well, it wasn't a Harley. But about your grandfather, more power. Your grandmother isn't the sweetest."

Arlene's head was pounding. She wanted to plug her ears, but she pressed on. What about his new wife, what was she like?

"His age, I think. She looks Jewish, but I'm bad at that. He does, too," she added thoughtfully. "Are *you* Jewish?"

"No." But Arlene felt a spark ignite. What if the silly girl was right? What if her grandfather had *not* been Protestant-from-the-North? What if *that* was why . . . why for generations they'd had to . . . after all, in those days, you didn't just . . . you couldn't hope to . . . the children would . . . it would be a terrible thing if . . . and so the children would feel . . . the father would have taken out his . . . naturally her mother would have had to . . . and as a small child you . . .

Arlene sat back, overwhelmed. Briefly she enjoyed the glow of revelation. Then she remembered the steamer records. The church records. The church! Of course they weren't Jewish.

The two boys came out with fries and ate while the girl wrote. It was growing dark. Under the table the simple-looking boy involved his leg with the girl's. He entwined them until he rocked the table, and then the girl kicked him and moved to another table.

"Simple," Arlene heard herself say. "We want things to be simple."

"This," Teresa said, pointing to her coffee, "is simply heavenly. I'd love another, but it must be time." It was after ten, and volunteers in fluorescent safety vests had blocked off traffic at Beach Avenue. "If only we had something besides Nabob Tradition Coffee," Teresa said. "Of all the kinds, why would you pick Tradition?" She sighed and leaned close. "I'll tell you why. We get Tradition because they're old. Yes. Most of them are." She fished in her bag. "I'll show you how old. See this? I found it on her dresser." She slapped down *12 Stories by Chekhov.* "Look when it was first published. That will give you an idea how old." She saw Arlene frowning. "Although to be fair I don't know if it's hers or her roommate's."

Roommate's? Someone watched her grandmother adjust her sleep-mask? Someone read "The Lady with the Dog" while her grandmother underlined important parts of the Bible with her blue pencil?

But Arlene did not have time to speak. There was a stream of people gliding down to the beach to watch the fireworks, and when the teenagers joined it, Teresa and Arlene followed them, again as if it were planned.

An old woman, a young woman, and a girl with two boys.

Drifting into eternity. No matter how she worded it, it made no sense to Arlene.

At the beach, they all fit on one log. The red-haired boy saw Teresa staring, and he offered her a drink. She thanked him.

"You guys think this body's over the hill," Teresa said to them all. "You watch." Her voice was affectionate. She emptied the cup and shook the last drops on the sand. "An old habit," she said.

"It's just beer," the fat boy complained. But the red-haired boy was impressed. "My name's Bernard," he said, offering her his hand. "Have you lived here long? From *Rupert*? I grew up there!"

Arlene began to feel like the oldest in the group, and this annoyed her. Also, there was something wrong with the fireworks. Some delay. The girl was still writing — now in complete darkness — but while this had at first fascinated, even charmed Arlene, now it was irritating. She considered asking the girl what she was writing when Bernard took a fresh can of beer from the bag. He held it between the girl's legs.

"Don't worry what others think of you, and don't worry about what you think of them. Or of yourself. Nobody knows anything . . . " the girl was writing, and then came the beer can. She slapped at it with her book; it bounced once, heavily, on the sidewalk behind her before it rose up in foam.

"Reverse psychology," Teresa said sympathetically. People were walking politely around the foaming can. The girl went on writing. "Will there be music for the fireworks?" Teresa asked Bernard. And turning to Michael, she said, "Why don't you find something good on your radio?"

Michael bent obediently over his tape player. "Something good for dancing," Teresa said.

Arlene tried to catch what a man was saying about a bomb threat. There would be fireworks but they'd be delayed.

Michael found a station playing "Stairway to Heaven." Teresa kicked off her shoes. "You can waltz to that, slow waltzing," she said, and held out her arms.

"Don't be envious of others when they have more than you do," the girl wrote. "Don't spoil their fun."

The old woman and the boy were cheek-to-cheek when the fireworks explosions began. It became clear that from where they were sitting explosions were pretty well all they would get: the sounds of bombing, and occasional sparkles along the tops of the trees.

Bernard and Teresa danced and the girl wrote in her notebook. Michael played DJ. He found a ballad from the 1970s which had been redone with a rap beat. A man yelled to turn off the music. "Just turn it down for a moment," Teresa said. "*That's* just like your grandmother," she said to Arlene, nodding at the man who had complained. "A real killjoy."

A killjoy? What about basic respect? Arlene was thinking. What about respect for the dead?

"Don't expect people to agree with what you like," the girl wrote.

Arlene felt inadequate, sitting beside the fat boy. She saw Teresa smiling, and suddenly Teresa was her grandmother after all. Her grandmother would have been happy to see Arlene dancing with Bernard. With somebody. With fat Michael? She looked at him again, and then at the girl writing in her notebook. That Nana would have frowned on. Writing a diary in public? It wasn't healthy. It surely wasn't attractive.

Suddenly one of the fireworks was different. It was gorgeous, and Bernard and Teresa must have sensed it, because they stopped dancing just in time to watch. When the last shooting stars exploded into smoke, and Teresa and Bernard were dancing again, Arlene recalled that her Nana's mother had died very young, and that her Nana had to take care of everyone in the family. All the younger brothers and sisters, and the father, and the house. When she was sixteen she had to teach school.

The rest of the fireworks were ordinary. The sky was full of smoke. When the dancers finally collapsed Arlene realized she was tense with waiting. She practically pounced on Teresa. "How old were you when you died?" she asked.

"Eighteen," gasped the old woman. She reached to Bernard for a beer.

"Did *you* have a grandmother?" Arlene asked. "Did you have someone who read to you? My grandmother used to read to us." She knew this sounded like bragging.

Teresa gulped from the can. "We've heard," she said. "She read you two books. One about a smart cat and the other about some children crawling around the attic."

The fireworks were over. If there had been anything spectacular at the end, they had missed it. But I know she loved me, Arlene was thinking. She smelled of roses all the time. Even if it was Avon. "Is she okay?" she asked. "Is she happy?"

Teresa sighed. "I think she likes it up there. She likes telling people what to do. Like *her*," she said loudly, so Bernard could hear, so even the girl herself had to look up. "She spends all her time making up rules."

"You're cynical for a teenager," Arlene said.

The old woman hooted. She was looking out at the freighters. "That's why I'm dead," she explained. She motioned for Arlene to lean down. "That boy," she whispered, nodding at Bernard. "When he gets older he's going to lose all that nice red hair. He'll look like everyone else." She sighed again.

Suddenly the dark-haired girl stood and began reading out her list of rules. Rules about diet and coupling and dealing with jealousy. Her voice gave the rules authority, even though taken all together they didn't sound practical, and it was difficult to hear her above the noise of families leaving the beach, kids setting off firecrackers.

Teresa hugged her tent-dress to her knees. She listened to half a dozen rules and then interrupted to ask if any of them applied to her, since she was dead.

"They'll all apply," the girl said. "Rules for the living apply to the dead." It was clear she didn't believe Teresa *was* dead. And why should she believe it?

Bernard and Michael were smirking, but Teresa began her lecture anyway. "You aren't interested, but I wasn't much older than you are now," she said to all of them. "And I wasn't any prettier. *And* my boyfriend didn't treat *me* well, either." She looked at Bernard, and her voice was apologetic. "Tonight was fun, but you *know* it's not right."

There was a silence. Then Bernard swiped at the girl's book and hurled it into the traffic.The girl jumped to get it, tripped, and lay still, winded. "Idiot," she said, breathing into the grass. She rolled over, pretended to be looking at the stars through the smoke. Then there was a space in time with no honking, no calling, no families, no laughter. It was as if no one was moving, or there were only animals — as if the human race had not yet come to earth. Everything on the planet was waiting for the girl to get her notebook back, or they had forgotten it altogether. Then a small dog came to snuffle at her face. The dog's owner called to it, sharply, the way he did when it strayed into a rosebush, and finally he gave the leash a tug, and the silly dog yelped, and leapt away, happy again.

NOT A DAY GOES BY

Lorne had a sleep and gave himself a careful shave before he drove out to the Derrick Golf and Country Club. He looked tired, but there was no need for people to guess he'd been driving all night and sleeping most of the day. Sixteen hours back from Vancouver. Ruth and Bill were having their party at the club; they were expecting him, although that wasn't why he'd driven straight back. What else could he have done?

Bill and Ruth were celebrating their fifteenth anniversary — the same number of years he and Janice had been married. They didn't know Janice had run off. Thursday morning at work he'd thought of telling Bill he was driving to Vancouver. But not to get his wife and kids — he'd never say that. So what was there to say?

That morning at work he'd been preoccupied with the details: he would need the chains; he should have taken the car in; he was worried about the shimmy. Bill took him to a restaurant for lunch — a family restaurant. He said he'd noticed Lorne hadn't remembered to bring his lunch for days, and Bill's wife Ruth was worried. Bill was grinning when he said this. He didn't miss a chance to let you know he was pleased with his wife.

They gave the young waitress their orders, and she smiled at them as if they were boys looking for trouble. Lorne felt a tingling across his hands and his neck as he gave her back the menu. He wasn't in cahoots with Bill or with anyone else. His wife had run off, that was all. People read into simple things, they never wanted to look at the facts.

He could have said something to Bill, then. Images took shape in his gut and moved up to his throat: Janice running off, the house, the noise the furnace made when the house was empty. *His* house, *his* furnace, and he was working still to pay for them.

But he kept quiet. It wasn't difficult. He knew Janice would be back. Maybe she was learning right now that you didn't run off from the home you'd made for your children. You didn't run off to people who had no love and no understanding — that was it, no understanding — you didn't run off to them with your three children.

Telling Bill and Ruth wasn't necessary; it would be an embarrassment when Janice got back.

In the beginning he expected her to walk in at any moment. She'd have the kids, but in his mind they were small again. Babies. He was so sure she'd be back that night or the next morning that he snacked on crackers, waiting. Crackers and sharp cheddar.

The next night he scrambled eggs in the Teflon fry pan the kids got her for Christmas. He remembered too late about using a plastic spatula. Libby's cat was meowing and walking through his legs; she wouldn't eat her cat chow. Finally he found liver in the freezer and hacked away at it, swearing. He cooked the slab in the fry pan when his eggs were done, then scraped an enormous serving into the cat's bowl. That stopped her whining. Some of the cooked liver went on the floor, and he planned to leave it for the cat to get. But some of it stuck to one of his moccasins and in the end it took longer to clean that and the streak on the living room rug than it would have taken to wipe the floor. Lorne wasn't a successful bachelor, he could admit that. But he was willing to reason things out, to learn from his mistakes. There was no reason a household shouldn't be as logical as one of the insurance policies he drafted at work.

And he could have been worse. Hadn't he remembered that his daughter's cat did not like dry cat chow? Didn't he know that his daughter was old enough now to use Kotex, and wouldn't he have bought them for her when she needed them?

The next night Janice wasn't back. He made eggs again and the liver smell came up from the scrapings in the frypan. He ate his meal standing over the stove, his shoulders drawn up and stiff.

He got through each day. He lay in bed and when the alarm went off he washed and shaved and went to work. He began to put in toast before he shaved and he ate it cold on his way out the door. He couldn't get anything else down. He found another loaf in the freezer, but Janice would be back before he'd gone through that. And there was still cereal.

He couldn't read the paper; he glanced over the financial section but he couldn't concentrate. He wasn't much of a bachelor, but everyone had a sorry story.

Nobody asked about Janice. Nobody knew her. They knew she was his wife, and after the open tournament in the summer Ruth had sat next to her at dinner. Ruth wore tight dresses and jewellery. If she thought Janice's outfit was plain, she was right. Lorne couldn't understand how Janice needed an entire afternoon to buy a dress that hung off her.

It was mild and snowing lightly when he parked at the club, and hot inside; Ruth and Bill had packed the lounge with people. Lorne golfed with a lot of them, and he knew some others from work. But it was easiest to stay close to Ruth, who started in right away about the duck pond they were putting in. Surely a big waste of money in Edmonton, but Lorne was nodding. He took crackers from the trays coming around. He was thinking about the weekend he'd had.

He had left work early on Thursday, coughing so that on Friday morning he would sound sick when he called from Vancouver. (When he called he was actually in North Vancouver, somewhere on the Dollarton Highway; he used a pay telephone so the call wouldn't be traced to his motel room. He felt the tingling in his hands again and worried he was about to tell the receptionist the whole story. That he was not sick in bed but standing at a gas station on the West Coast. That he had spent the last hour driving around Mount Seymour in an unbelievable fog. That he'd been looking for the Tripps' house with a map that made no sense. He was afraid he'd tell the receptionist about Harvey Tripp, who was married to Janice's sister and had a screw loose.)

He'd been prepared for Harvey Tripp and his screwy ideas, but he hadn't counted on the look his own little girl gave him. What kind of look was that for a twelve-year-old girl to have? Once he'd seen what Janice's brainwashing had done to Libby he didn't want to see the boys.

That made him a quitter. He admitted that. He wished there was someone who could understand what he had done and what he had been unable to do but it wasn't Bill or Ruth. No one at this party had that kind of understanding in them. Maybe a priest or a preacher would understand. Someone must know what he didn't know. He was a failure if he didn't know how to keep his family together. He'd driven back to Edmonton alone. He was a failure. He admitted that.

Ruth teased him for being a bachelor at their wedding anniversary dinner, but she was sympathetic when he told her Janice had been up all night with the boys. A flu. Ruth smiled; the boys and Libby were old enough not to need a sitter but Ruth understood, she would have done the same thing as Janice. "You can't have got much sleep yourself," she said.

In short, the idea that Lorne premeditated hurting Ruth and Bill's daughter was nonsense. He wasn't thinking about Erica, he was thinking about his own little girl. Sure, they were the same age. He knew that. He'd driven them home from the pool, dropped Erica at her front door, waited to see she had her key. In his opinion there wasn't much to like. She was a skinny thing and she was disrespectful. Bill seemed to let that go.

Bill was losing his hair and he let that go too. Hair all over his sweater. Everyone got older but you could take some care. Lorne did what he could. When he had time he bent over and brushed the hair he had left for fifty strokes. He ate raw garlic to stimulate the follicles.

Bill was a character. He let his wife run the show. Most days he called her before he left work so she could give him a list of things to do on the way home. Everyone in the office could hear and Bill didn't care about that either.

It was true that later on Lorne had, in fact, hit Erica, but it wasn't deliberate, he certainly didn't intend to hurt her. He hit her with a door. Off the lounge was a hall with the Men's and further on the Ladies', and Erica was standing in front of the Men's. Lorne asked her did she know she was in a public place, did she know she was standing outside the men's washroom, that any man could come out and without meaning to walk into her or swing the door open and hit her? Hit her a lot harder than he had.

No, she didn't know that, and no, no one had taught her how to behave in a public place. She was shaking her head, she wouldn't say anything, wouldn't talk to him. You had to wonder if she was all there, hiding behind a bathroom door when people coming in and out couldn't help but hit her.

He didn't know why Bill and Ruth had brought her along. It was nearly midnight; surely they could have hired a sitter. But that was their affair. He remembered feeling restless after the meal, when the toasting began. They toasted Bill and Ruth because it was their party. It turned out they were young with their fifteen-year-old marriage; there were couples who had been married twenty-five years and they had to make speeches, too. Then there were couples married thirty years. They all took their turns and then they wanted to know who'd been married thirty-five years, and then who'd been married the longest of all.

Lorne needed some air, so he went to see how the new pool was coming. They would end up wanting to know who planned to stay married the longest, and after that who wasn't yet married but planned to get married and then stay married the longest.

That was nonsense too. Lorne hadn't planned to be married. He hadn't planned not to either. He thought he might get married and raise a family and he did. He was still married. When Janice came back she would have to look at what she meant, running off to her sister's, running off with the kids in the middle of the school year. He didn't regret marrying Janice. That's not what he was saying. It would have been fifteen years for him and Janice, the same as it was for Ruth and Bill.

He had a lot on his mind that evening but it wasn't Erica. There had to be something smart about Erica if Libby wanted to be her friend. But she had that stubbornness, a kind of arrogance. Libby came home from playing at her house and told her mother that Erica's mother had a television in the kitchen and a mirror above the sink so she could watch TV while she was ironing or doing the dishes.

"Is that it?" Lorne asked when Janice told him. "Is that what you want? A television you can watch while you're doing the dishes?"

"No, Lorne, I don't want that," Janice said.

"Then let's not hear any more about Erica's mother watching the TV while she does the dishes," Lorne said.

After that Libby didn't play at Erica's. He didn't say she couldn't; she just had the good sense not to. Lorne still went over if Bill and Ruth were having cocktails but Janice said she had just the one good dress and it showed the bruises, so Lorne usually said she wanted to stay home with the kids.

In the fall when he'd first started at Sun Life with Bill they often worked late and sometimes Ruth brought dinner — fluffy things with names like Potato Dream. She used too much salt and mayonnaise but she was cheerful and she liked to stay a few minutes while they ate. "To make sure you don't keep talking about premiums," she said. What about summer holidays? she wanted to know. Why not rent cabins together at the lake?

Lorne said that sounded grand, but he told Janice to tell her the next time they were on the telephone that they preferred to camp. Janice didn't tell him she never talked with Ruth on the telephone. It didn't matter; Ruth stopped bringing it up.

In the morning Bill and Ruth were taking the train to Lake Louise. This was what Bill told them all in his speech. He said it was a shame they couldn't have held their anniversary party at Lake Louise. After he was done it was Ruth's turn. She looked at Bill and said they were going to be alone with the bears in the mountains, cut off from civilization for two weeks. They'd better feast their eyes now, she said. Everybody laughed. Lorne supposed they were laughing at the notion of Edmonton being civilized. Lorne laughed because it was easy for him to do the right thing in a situation, it had always been easy. But he was thinking that Lake Louise was hardly cut off; nobody roughed it in those hotels.

The first thing he saw on his tour was the receptionist. It wasn't the girl Libby hung around when the family went out to the club on Sundays. That was Susan. Libby read Susan all her stories and poems and Susan gave her paper with the country club letterhead. Lorne didn't know where Janice was when this was going on, why she wasn't taking care of Libby.

He remembered thinking then about the game they used to play together, although that still had nothing to do with Erica. It was when Libby was small, a fat little tadpole. He lay on the bed and pulled his knees up and got her balanced on his feet. Then he threw her in the air. Not too high, a few inches, but she screamed every time, she was delighted. Delighted.

The first time he was over at Ruth and Bill's he told Erica he'd show her a good game, and Ruth looked at him sideways, sharply. But he wouldn't have wanted to show Erica any game, not even how to skip stones. She was like a stone herself. She wouldn't know how to have a good time. Ruth was a good wife but she didn't know what made little girls happy.

Libby had been a fat little tadpole. She screamed, "Stop, Daddy! Daddy, stop!" Her eyes got a wild look because she liked to think their game was dangerous, as dangerous as it was for her big brothers to prowl in the woods by the river.

He nodded to the receptionist and looked down over the scaffolding where the new pool was going to be. Then he walked across to the TV lounge. There were some young people watching a religious program. After Janice ran off he'd watched one just because of the preacher. The preacher's eyes, and something about his hands and the way he leaned toward the audience. It reminded Lorne of himself. Mostly the eyes. Lorne could be charming. He made people laugh, but they also took him seriously. He was tall and had good shoulders and he knew he was direct. Janice said his eyes flickered from grey to blue when he was angry. Before they were married they took a picnic to the river by Black Mud and a storm came up. It was a great chance to huddle under a tree while it blew over. She told him then that he had stormy eyes, and he studied himself in the mirror and saw she was right.

He wanted to watch the preacher so he would know more about himself and how people saw him. Janice had told him some people might feel intimidated. They might suspect he knew things they didn't know, things that might be good for him but bad for them. "Do *you* think that?" he'd asked her, but she said no, it was something a person who didn't know him well might think. Or a person who was insecure. They might feel threatened.

When he got back to the party they had finished the speeches and people were getting refills. Lorne was thinking that the preachers on television sounded like simpletons but that didn't stop anyone from believing them, so it wasn't a matter of intelligence or charisma. It had a lot to do with what you yourself brought to the television. Your secret wishes and your needs. You did a magic trick: you changed a hick into a man of god.

You had to wonder what might happen if someone with a great deal of intelligence got on the television and did the same thing. There was money to be made there.

There's nothing you know that will help me, mister, Lorne remembered thinking. He remembered saying it to himself. It was the only way he could talk himself into changing channels after Janice had run off. "There's nothing you know that could possibly help a man like me," he said again.

Now he would have found that ridiculous. He wouldn't have watched for five seconds. He returned to the party, and stood chewing olives until Ruth was beside him.

"Lorne, *who* are you calling mister, are you calling me mister?" she said. "Are you drinking tonight, are you a free agent?"

"Free as a bird," Lorne said. Ruth thought it was Janice who kept him from booze.

"That's grand." Ruth waved at the girl to bring the tray.

Lorne *was* drinking for a change. He got hangovers, but tonight it seemed worth it to get one rather than explain. On that count he preferred Ruth to Bill: you could tell Ruth you were feeling off and she would leave you alone, but Bill had to know what it was you had. He wouldn't drop it. It happened every time they were working late, and finally he said, "Bill, you don't ask God why *He's* not drinking. Because He doesn't need to! A fool needs to drink to say what he has to say. I can say anything I want, Bill, and so can you."

That stopped Bill, but the next time Lorne went over for cocktails Bill pushed him again. Lorne had to tell him about the all-day hangovers he got. Sometimes two days. "They're out of this world, Bill," he said.

"I can appreciate that," Bill said, but then he had to go on.

"Those aren't hangovers, they're migraines," he said. "Usually it's women who get them but not always."

"Whatever," Lorne said.

Lorne didn't know if he'd been in an unusual frame of mind when he arrived at the party. It wasn't every weekend he drove sixteen hours straight with no chains through the mountains in a car with a shimmy. He was going to pick up Libby and Joey and Jack from their schools. There was no point seeing Janice first. He had to be prepared for a wild reaction from Janice and her sister. They would get Tripp to talk to him. To stop him from driving out to the childrens' schools. Janice would be worried. It was time she did some worrying if she wanted to call herself a mother. What kind of mother left her children in a motel room in the middle of an Edmonton winter while she stood at the desk talking to her sister on the West Coast to see if she could run off there? That's what she was doing when he drove in. When he finally found the two-bit motel she'd taken them to. What kind of mother was that?

His plan was to drive all night, get to Vancouver just before rush hour (he hoped) and then sleep until one or two — give himself time to have a shower and shave before he drove to the schools. He didn't want the kids to think he looked like a madman. They'd have been staying with Janice's sister. He'd pick them up at their schools at three o'clock and offer to drive them back to the Tripps'. He'd talk to Janice there. If he could be with all of them, if they could be together, she would see she'd made a mistake and she would come home. They could stay over one last night, then drive back to Edmonton on Saturday. Be back in time for Ruth and Bill's fifteenth on Sunday.

What did happen was different. The garage didn't have time to look at the car and he'd worried about the shimmy until he was into the mountains. Then he worried about not having chains. With the family he would have stopped somewhere in the

Okanagan, but he went straight through. He was on the Hope-Princeton before he began to feel tired.

He got out by a creek to stretch his legs. The air was cold and pure. It made him think of Libby. How could you do it, Daddy? He looked over the mountains, and everything was dead, it was all rock. It wasn't a matter of choosing. In this life you did what you had to do. He wondered if everything had been a dream, if he had a family at all. It was one of those thoughts you can get when you're tired. At that moment it had seemed that everything true must be there with him in the mountain night: his stiff back, his stale breath, the Rambler. The rest was fantasy. He got back in the car and sat wishing he still smoked. He even looked through the glove compartment for an old deck. It came to him that he must have a family. Why else would he work all day for a few almighty dollars in a job that ground him down?

In Hope he turned on the radio and learned it was four in the morning, not five. He turned off to have a sleep, but he was too nervous for that. He kept thinking about the morning rush hour traffic into Vancouver if he didn't get in by seven-thirty. He pulled back onto the highway and drove. The traffic was light when he got to Vancouver and he had a chance to look over the Fraser River from the bridge and see the other bridges and a bit of the way the city was being developed. It was a pretty city but he couldn't see why Harvey Tripp wanted to live on the north shore with all the rain.

He drove straight up to Second Narrows and took the first exit off the bridge. At each intersection he looked at the map but before he figured out where he was on the Dollarton highway he saw a motel. He pulled in. It was half past eight. He took off his shirt and slacks and lay down in his undershirt and slept on and off until noon.

It was kids yelling outside the window that woke him. Finally he looked through the drapes and saw they were Indian kids.

Maybe that's who Libby's friends were now, Indian kids. Janice wouldn't bother to stop her. Probably the Tripp children had always played with Indian kids.

He shaved and bought a map showing the schools and he circled the most likely ones. It was possible that Janice wasn't at her sister's anymore but he assumed she was. She wouldn't want the kids to change schools again. He and Janice had always agreed on the children's education. He didn't know what Janice had to complain about. She had everything she needed. There was nothing they couldn't have worked out between them. She had a tendency to get hysterical. Sometimes he told her she should see a psychiatrist but there was probably no cure for it, it was her personality.

He had a grilled cheese sandwich in the motel coffee-shop and drove to the school he thought was Libby's. He had not been in a school for years; Janice went to the parent-teacher nights. They had good kids, there was never anything the teachers had to tell them. One teacher told Janice he had tried everything but he didn't know what to do with Libby. Lorne thought the teacher must be a goof, but he made Libby look up the word courtesy in the dictionary.

The ceilings in this school were low. He supposed they were low in all the new schools but he thought Libby might like this one because there was art work up in the halls.

Most of the classroom doors were closed but the grade seven door was open. He heard Libby before he saw her. She was with another girl; they were playing a game on the blackboard. There was no one else in the room. He stood in the doorway a moment. Libby wrote an S on a large sloping grid they'd drawn. Then her friend turned and then Libby turned and her mouth fell open. She made a whimpering sound and ran past him with her arms drawn up. She pushed by him and ran down the hall screaming. "Mr. Dawes, it's my father, my father's here." Classroom doors were opening as he followed her down the hall to the principal's office.

Lorne was doing his best to drink heavily. He watched the hostess make her way through the groups to the bar and he felt his lip curl. He knew he did that because his kids started doing it in the car this last summer. He turned and slapped Joey when he saw him in the rearview mirror, but then Libby sulked all the way to Penticton. Libby took up the cause of her brothers if she thought they'd been wronged. If she saw an injustice.

"You have nothing to sulk about," he told her at the campsite. But she stood still as a statue, just her lips moving, "You do it all the time, Daddy, that's why Joey does it, because you do."

All the time? You didn't doubt that she kept track. She watched them all. She was a smart little girl. He couldn't hug her then because that would confuse them, make them think he was like Bill.

All the time? He was certainly doing it now, he could feel his lip curling. The day after Janice ran off he didn't go in to the office; he didn't even call because he had nothing to say. He spent the day in the bathroom reading financial journals and trying to catch himself in the mirror. He imagined himself with different people to see how his face looked and if his lip curled. He tried to feel the signs of it coming on.

Now he smiled because Ruth was walking toward him. He told her she had bewitched him, there was no other explanation for the way he was drinking. "You've be-whitched me," he said, adding a little gust of air. "I'm high as a kite."

Ruth was talking about their garden. They were having problems. Ruth wore her black hair in a braid like a young girl, and bright red lipstick. He was curious about her.

"Does Ruth think she's a girl?" he had once asked Janice.

"I don't know," Janice said.

"I know you don't know," he said, "but you must have some idea, you're a woman."

"I think she doesn't like to wear make-up," Janice finally said. "I don't know why but there are some women who don't. It stings their cheeks, some of the powders can, though I don't know why. I always think it feels lovely and smooth."

"All right," Lorne had said. "I don't want a big production."

Ruth was Polish or Czech and so plain he'd wondered what Bill had seen in her. Now he wondered if Bill hadn't been the smart one. Her face was plain, but she had a great figure and she knew how to dress, and she was at ease in the club lounge. She could have been in her own living room. She made sure the waitresses brought drinks and she kept things going and talked with the oddballs. And where was Janice? At the foot of Seymour Mountain.

Ruth was telling him they'd found the neighbour boy going through Bill's tools in the shed. He was supposed to be digging the hole for their duck pond.

Maybe the boy needed some tools, Lorne said.

"Tools to dig a duck pond? Oh, Lorne! You're not even listening!" Ruth cried.

Lorne excused himself and then realized he did need to use the facilities. He remembered feeling drunk and a little dizzy and taking extra care. That's where the girl came in. She was standing behind the door when he came out of the Men's; you'd think she wanted to get hit. He took the time to stop and tell her that she should find another place to play and she looked as if she couldn't figure out what the words meant.

Was she going to stand there all night in front of the Men's restroom, was that it? When she wouldn't answer he told her he was going to take her back to her parents. The short way, around the front, he said, and he took her arm. He had to pull a little to get her moving. He didn't want this skinny thing hopping along beside him but he couldn't leave her there in front of the Men's. "Your parents are waiting," he said to hurry her up. When they passed the main entrance he had a craving for fresh air and he pulled her outside. He looked at the quiet snow falling on the cars in the parking lot and the girl asked if he was going to have a cigarette. He said no, but he wished he were. If he'd had one he would have smoked it.

He wanted to take advantage of the fact that the girl was warming up to him. "Did my wife tell you not to speak to me?" he asked her. "I'm not a stranger. I'm a friend of your parents." But the girl had turned back to stone. He leaned against the wall. He didn't dare close his eyes because of the dizziness. Why had Libby run to the principal? Run from her own father, her high little voice screaming, "Mr. Dawes, it's my father, my father's here!"

He had planned to take them out to the A&W. Maybe they'd rather go to McDonald's. He liked the root beer at the A&W, that was all. But Dawes phoned Janice's sister and got her to come pick Libby up. Everything was spoiled. Lorne found the high school but now things were ruined; Libby wasn't in the front seat beside him. He missed the entrance to the parking lot so he pulled over across the street. A group of kids stood by the bushes, smoking, and after a moment he realized they were watching him. He drove off.

He drove until he came to a mall. He found a booth and called Janice's sister. Harvey Tripp answered and he got an earful from him so he gave him an earful back. But that didn't stop Harvey Tripp. "Lorne, you need to get help," he remembered him saying. "Here's a number you can call."

"You can shove your number," Lorne said. "You're the nut."

Harvey Tripp and his wife were coddling their children. They were spoiling their girl but they were coddling the boy too, turning him into a homosexual. Lorne didn't need to call any number Harvey Tripp gave him. So he drove back to Edmonton. Got back ahead of schedule and without his family. Slept and woke up and showered and shaved and now he was at an anniversary party. End of story.

A light wind came up. The snow was swirling, but he hadn't let go of the girl's hand and so she was still standing there beside him. "Do you want to find your parents?" he asked her. "Did your parents ever tell you to stay put if you got lost? That's good advice, did they tell you that?"

The girl wouldn't answer. He was trying to make his voice sugar but he felt the anger bulging in his head.

"Don't worry," he said. "I know where your parents are." He had to pull at her to get her to come in out of the cold. She couldn't have weighed more than eighty pounds but she made herself into a dead weight. He realized when they got inside that he'd have to walk her around a bit to warm her up or her parents would wonder what had happened. "We'll take another short-cut," he said.

His head was light as air; he imagined that he was in the tropics and had nothing to do but lie on the beach. At the same time he felt he had in front of him a fantastically complex safe to crack. Inside the safe were millions of dollars. He felt free as a bird. He had nowhere to be by nine o'clock the next morning and no boys to put through college. No mortgage. He had no plan in his head. Erica was a sulky girl and if she'd been his he would have given her a paddling, but she couldn't spoil his good mood now.

She looked up at him like she thought he was going to take out a gun. Did Libby tell her things at school? What kinds of things was Janice telling the kids? He didn't know. He didn't even know what Janice had told Libby and the boys.

He doubted that Janice had ever wanted to be a mother. There was nothing he could have done about that, though, no way he could have known about that before he married her.

"I want to go back," Erica said. He hadn't expected her to say anything. He smiled down at her but she wouldn't smile back.

He felt his patience thin out. He gripped her hand and said, "Do you think your mommy and daddy love you? Is that what you think?"

The girl wouldn't nod or even look at him now. She screwed up her eyes and stood on one foot and then the other. She was pretending to concentrate on something down at the end of the hall when there was nothing there and when all he wanted was for her to look at him directly, to look at him. "You think your parents love you, is that it? Is that the story?" He thought she might say yes, even a whisper, but she wouldn't say anything and her eyes were wide now, staring. He grabbed her arm. It wasn't much thicker than his wrist, and it was as cold as her hand. She wouldn't say anything, and he didn't know what else he could do so he gave her arm a twist. He remembered her whimper, and he thought afterward that it was possible she had twisted her body in such a way that it broke her arm. He couldn't think of any other moment when she could have broken it. It was easy to break your arm when you were a kid. His own boy had broken his arm falling from the swings.

The last thing he expected was for her to run off. When she did he lunged but he didn't go after her for a moment because he was so surprised. She disappeared into the locker area and he realized she was going to go whining to her parents. He sprinted and caught up to where she should have been, but she had hidden. That was all right. There was no door at the end. Eventually she would have to give herself up.

He flattened himself against the lockers, listening to his own heart beat. He noticed he wasn't breathing. Only his heart was beating. He felt like a man from a new race that needed no oxygen; possibly he was onto something that the scientists were just discovering in their labs. He would always be optimistic; there would always be doomsday prophets and people who thought they were hard done by, but the only reason they were hard done by was they had no backbone. So she was hiding, the little snip.

He heard a bump. It didn't take long to find the locker; there was a density in the air around it, body heat, it must have been, coming from the slats. He was grinning when he swung open the door.

"Now you're talking," he said. "There's more than one way to skin a cat. So you think your mommy and daddy love you."

The girl's lips were covered with snot and he had to push her back in the locker because he hadn't expected that and he didn't know what to do with her. A few months back Janice had begged him not to use the golf clubs but she wouldn't talk, there was no other way to get anything out of her, nothing sensible, anyway, and he had to keep swinging at her. That only made her speak in gibberish and he couldn't get her to stop that either. He swung at her and she wouldn't stop and finally they were both quiet. She was bleeding and had snot on her face and she was certainly a dead weight. He had one hell of a time getting her cleaned up in the car outside Emergency.

Now he stood trying to think what to do. It occurred to him that the girl would be at eye-level with the slats. If ever there had been a moment when he wished he could start his life over and do things differently, it was now. But he already had his watch off. He threaded the worn leather through the lock loops.

"This is a special lock, Erica, because I want to keep you safe. If you break this lock a special alarm will go off and the security police will come and take you away. Don't try to break the lock, Erica."

That was it. Oh, yes, there was one more thing he remembered: that his rubber soles gripped the floor enough to make a little sucking sound as he stepped back.

Sure he wanted to see his kids. He thought about them all the time. Not a day went by that he didn't think about them. What had Janice been saying?

CROWS

Vianne was only half listening to Jody read; it was fifteen minutes to closing, and she wanted the man with the wings to look over. Jody held a barrette between her teeth, making the prediction sound dangerous: "Leo. Count on a brief identity crisis. Emerge with renewed sense of purpose. Family unity provides support. Does that sound right?" Jody snapped the barrette shut on her braid.

Jody's family was thick as peanut butter over the city, hundreds of them, waiting for each others' crises so they could be there. This was how Vianne pictured it. Her own family was small, and she was the only survivor. The others had died in a plane crash on their way home from a family reunion. Vianne was alive only because she had not gone to the reunion. She told people who didn't know better that she'd been writing exams; the fact was, she had no good reason.

Now she pulled at her own flat hair as she answered Jody's question. "Support . . . there was tension. A kind of support if you're a plankton."

Jody tugged her braid down through the barrette. It was Vianne's use of the word "drowned." That was what Vianne's whole family had done after the crash. Vianne uncrossed her thin arms and let them swing. She was all right. Keeping busy helped. Helping others was the key; she was considering giving talks in community centres.

The man with the wings came into the library most days near closing to read the bulletin board. He wore black wings and a black mask with a black beak. Sometimes he wore black jeans and then the whole get-up was black. He was wise to choose an all-black outfit. If his beak had been yellow, people would laugh. Black was the answer if you wanted to dress like a bird and still be taken seriously.

The birdman always read the entire board. He was two-thirds done now, and had out a notebook. The evening light danced slick and yellow over his wings as he wrote. It was spring going on summer. Who wouldn't want to fly around?

"Do you think those feathers are real?" Jody whispered.

"Sure," Vianne said. "I had an uncle who tried to fly off a building with pigeon wings. He sewed hundreds of them together. It made headlines but it wasn't an isolated incident, a lot of people did it in the late sixties."

The crow-man pulled his arms back under his wings and left the library. Perhaps his neck was longer than average, and his head jutted forward — although it could have been the beak giving it this front-heaviness — but otherwise, he had manly shoulders and legs. He was manly in the way you'd expect the cutest boys in elementary school to turn out. Why was it that they never did? Diet. A lack of exercise. Weak genes. Or lead poisoning. The possibilities were endless. But did he really want to be a bird?

Later in the week a woman came in to photocopy articles on the massacre. She brought the papers up and counted out change. "I hate being a human being," she said. "They're trivializing it. They're . . . "

"I know." Vianne was colour-coding books with gummed dots. The birdman had not come in. "My brother did something like that," she said. "But it was a while ago. Are you finished with the articles?"

The woman's eyes narrowed. "Your brother . . . ? Sorry, I didn't hear . . . "

"Well, not quite the same. A multiple molester. One after the other. Twelve-year-olds at first, but they got younger."

The woman looked at the pile of quarters and dimes she had just counted out.

"I called them Lolita the First, and so on. He didn't like to be teased and he stopped telling me. But I knew. You know that look people get?"

After the woman left the change and backed out the door, Jody burst out of the office. Jody liked scenes. "You've never suffered," she said now. "You've never known sorrow. Your type — " and she nodded at the bulletin board, because there he was with his wings, a third of the way through the notices — "You're so self-centred." She knocked a stack of filing cards together. Vianne was wondering about pizza. With anchovies or without? "I've heard your stories," Jody said darkly. "You should thank God you're alive."

You had to be in the mood for anchovies. In fact Vianne was not in the mood for pizza. She would pick up pasta. There was a Safeway across from the library. She knew where everything was and she could buy a week's groceries in ten minutes. Ahead of her on the way out was a student with a black clingy outfit and an expensive black leather book bag. As the student passed the food bank she dropped a can into the side pocket of her bag, and Vianne hurried after her, wondering if dogs felt this pleased when they had something to follow. Vianne compared the African violets while the girl flirted with the boy filling the plant display, and after a moment she interrupted them.

"I couldn't help seeing how you took that can from the food bank," she said.

The girl looked around. "What are you talking about? I don't know her," she told her friend.

Her friend unpacked another plant. "Rachel wouldn't take anything from the food bank. She's loaded."

"Definitely," said Rachel.

Vianne smiled at the young man, whose pin said "Brad." He was one of the boys you didn't notice in grade five. "Why don't you look in her bag, Brad?"

Brad put down a mum. It was raining now, and the air was filled with the hissing of car tires. Brad put his hand into the bag and carefully lifted out a can of flaked light tuna. Rachel made a choking sound.

"I'm not clairvoyant, but I pick up on these things," Vianne explained. "My twin sister's a klepto. She trafficks in forgeries — the Great Masters. She wouldn't tell *me*, I just see it in the papers. And she started out in Safeway, just like you. I think she went on to A&B Sound. Safeway was too easy. I think she felt pathetic — well, don't you? Stealing from the food bank? How long do you plan to stay with it?" Vianne left Rachel crying and Brad holding the tuna.

The man with wings never took out books. Finally one day Vianne joined him at the bulletin board and asked if she could help him. Was he looking for anything in particular? "Yes — I'm looking for crow get-togethers," he told her.

Vianne told him that was like her cousin, who organized seances. Spiritual get-togethers, he called them, but when they got to his house he kept them prisoner for the whole weekend and did weird tests on them. He made them listen to tapes that said, "I am a horrible useless person and nobody will ever want to spend five minutes with me." "Seventy-two hours straight with nothing but carrot juice and they couldn't go to the bathroom," Vianne said. "No, they could go. I'm mixing it up with something else."

It was impossible to guess the crow-man's expression with that mask, but he waved one of his wings in a friendly way. "I'm just looking for birds of a feather," he said.

"You're never going to find a notice for a crow get-together."

Then Vianne remembered how glad she had been to see him come into the library. "Try going down to the beach," she said. "Go down after a storm. That's when you see the most crows — they're after all the dead things that get washed up."

"I'm not a carrion crow," the man said.

"But you eat garbage, don't you?"

"So do you."

Vianne paused. "I don't know much about crows," she said finally.

"No? I could tell you . . . "

"Sure. And I'll tell you about my family." Vianne winked and went back to her desk to get ready for closing.

A few minutes after she got in her door there was a knock. It was the crow-man. He still had the whole outfit on, including the mask. This made her notice his legs. They were the legs of a twenty-year-old: he should be out running on a night like this, not standing like a pin-up against her porch railing.

"I wanted to ask if you had anything shiny," he said. "That you didn't need."

"You followed me!"

"I wanted to give you time to go to the bathroom. Women always go when they first get anywhere. Also before they go out."

"Does that go for women crows?"

"I don't know any."

Vianne laughed with him. "What's in the toolbox?" It was on the railing beside him.

"Tools."

Vianne nodded, and she felt a shiver of desire that was perhaps not so odd: he did have strong-looking legs and a warm voice. He might be ugly underneath the mask, but she doubted it.

She invited him in, and tried not to notice how he checked out her kettle, the spring on her study lamp, the hinges on the fridge. Damn that mask: how was she supposed to know if he was just *acting* like a crow? She found an old pot at the back of a cupboard. She had gone out and left the stove on and the bottom had adhered to the element. The crow-man looked pleased with her gift.

Then he told her about the Great Crow. The Great Crow had come down to earth and made man and woman, but he had grown annoyed with them because they were killing off more buffalo than they needed. So he took away the sun. Then his brother felt sorry for the people and brought the sun down to them. The problem was, the brother was too tired to get back up to the sky.

"I'm his brother," the crow-man explained.

"The brother of the Great Crow?"

"Uh, yes, but another brother."

"Another brother?"

"Not the one who brought the sun back."

"Oh. *Another* brother!" Vianne was laughing now. She went to put the kettle on, and she stood in the hiss of the gathering steam. There was a difference between eccentric and plain crazy, but at present she could not think what it was. And it was nice to have company, to laugh a little. She fluffed her hair and looked at the kettle to put on more lipstick. "Why don't you take off the mask," she said casually, when she came back with the tray.

"Okay. But first give me your impressions." The crow-man walked around shaking his wings out.

"Fit," Vianne said immediately. "Very fit for a crow. You must work out."

"I walk a lot. Okay, I'll jump in. You want to be noticed. That's why you put on more lipstick. Sorry. I notice colour. I don't mean to embarrass you. It looks nice."

"My turn: you're . . . an introverted extrovert." Vianne patted her cheeks to draw away the colour. "And lonely."

"We're all lonely," the crow-man said.

"Not like you," Vianne said.

"Ah. So you know me?" He took off his mask and Vianne got

the surprise of her life: it was Garnet Christiansen! She and Shelly Wong used to stand on the hill watching his house with binoculars.

"Garnet — the cutest boy in grade five!" Even better looking now; his features had lengthened and his skin had the wrinkles that made you think of strong character rather than old age.

"Well," Garnet said.

"Oh, you were! And you knew it. I'll bet you didn't think I was cute then."

"No, but I do now."

"Oh."

"And with my luck," Garnet said, "you did then but you don't now, right?"

Vianne said it was unfair. Garnet had been coming to the library for weeks; he had talked to her, seen her face, while she had only just now seen his. Then she noticed his ring finger.

"You aren't wearing the ruby ring we gave you," she said. "I got to put it in your desk. We couldn't find garnet."

Garnet frowned, then smiled, nodding.

"You were such a hero. Remember you admitted you shoved Chris Zelinsky's coat in the garbage?"

"No . . . "

"Yes! Ball made the whole class stay in, all lined up, one by one we had to talk with the principal. Did they find out who peeled the orange on top?"

"I don't know. I didn't say I did it, though."

"Oh. But after you came out he let us go."

Garnet shrugged. "He probably wanted to go home."

There was a silence. "Well, you look like you're in good shape," Vianne said. "You don't fly, do you?"

Garnet shook his head. He walked a lot, all over the city, his wings were only decorative.

"But you think you come from the sky. That myth you told me."

"I suppose. When I think about it. We all have some sort of creation myth. Where do you think you come from, the primordial ooze?"

Vianne hesitated to discuss her religious convictions with someone who believed he came from the crows. Even if he had been in her grade five class. As soon as he left, she went into the bathroom to make sure the hand mirror was still there. Then she French-braided her blond hair into two pigtails, the way she had in grade five. She wiped off her eyeliner and lipstick, and squinted, and there was the grinning girl she had been for the school photographer.

Garnet came in earlier than usual the next day, and after he had finished with the bulletin board he came to the desk to chat. Vianne invited herself over to his house, and when he said it was too messy she decided to follow him. It took an hour to walk half a dozen blocks because Garnet kept stopping at houses along the way. As far as she could make out he only went into the kitchens. Sometimes he went in through the window, but most of the time the doors were unlocked. After he'd come out of one kitchen he stood by the garage in the alley rearranging his pack to make more room. Then he turned to the salal bush.

"I know you're with me, Vianne," he said. "I don't mind, but I've got one more place to go to. Then we can go put our feet up."

Vianne expected his suite to be a scrap heap, but apart from the two kettles, the cutlery and the stainless steel pot he unloaded, there was not a shiny thing in sight. "I get migraines," he explained. "Reflected light can trigger one just like that. That's why I wear the mask." He took it off and showed her the Polaroid sunglasses he had moulded into the papier-mâché. Then he pushed a button by the telephone and the back wall went up on tracks along the ceiling. The space behind was as large as the room itself and filled with neat pyramids of metal objects: filing cabinets, toasters, bird cages, woks.

"This is pathological," Vianne said.

"I know." Garnet found a place to perch his new kettles and pot and he filed the cutlery in a series of cookie tins. Then he put the wall up again and nodded to his answering machine. The light was blinking six times.

The messages, he explained, were from his mother, who would want to know if he was coming for dinner on Sunday. He did not listen to the messages, but when there were seven he knew it was Sunday and time to go. "A great device for crows. We aren't good at time," he said. "We're more general: winter, summer, that kind of thing."

Vianne nodded. "So are you going? To your mother's tomorrow?"

"If tomorrow's Sunday. I take my laundry. She gives me homemade bread and jam."

"With a mother like that, you have no right to be crazy."

"Why? Doesn't your mother ever give you homemade jam?"

"Yes. Raspberry." Vianne was whispering. She did not want to say another word. "My mother," she said, "is like that shiny stuff. No matter how quickly I think about her, I get a pain."

They sat a moment on the couch.

"If we have no right to be crazy, why are we crazy? Wouldn't you rather do something else than stand around the bulletin board in a bird suit?"

"You're right. Let's clean up," Garnet said. "I'll get rid of all the junk. And I do think you're pretty. What do you like most? What do you really love?"

"Pussywillows." Vianne said it and then a lot of other things came into her mind, but it was too late.

"Pussywillows?"

He kissed her.

They made a pact. "No more showing up in the library with the wings," he said.

"No more horror stories," Vianne said.

She was tested the next day when a woman came into the library and asked Vianne how her uncle was.

"My uncle?"

"The one who . . . the abuser."

"Oh, fine!" Vianne declared. Then she called the woman back and explained that she had made it up. She was sorry she troubled to confess.

"I don't think it's funny," the woman said.

Later, Vianne hung around Jody's desk, reading memos upside down and pulling tacks from the paper clip magnet. When Jody finally told her to quit messing things up she blurted out the apology she had memorized. She was sorry she had told so many lies right there in the library. "You were right," she said. "I've never known sorrow. I can't even imagine what Jesus must have felt like on the cross. I understand that for you Catholics the main thing . . . " She paused. This territory had nothing to do with the apology, but it was cozy. "The main thing wasn't how the nails felt, but what gravity did. Suffocated him. But it was different for him, because he *wanted* to be there suffering. I just want to have fun."

Jody ignored this and pointed to the pussywillows on the counter. "Where did you get those? That bird guy rip them off?"

Vianne leaned close to whisper. "'He is my grade five lover," she said. "We are going to stay together forever."

It turned out Jody was right about Garnet stealing the pussywillows. But this was not exactly breaking the pact, because they were not shiny. And in every other way Garnet was doing all right. Six months passed, and they were almost sure Vianne was pregnant. They were saving for a downpayment on an apartment, and Garnet suggested he lift a few things. Just from the easy houses.

"I don't like the idea either," Garnet said, looking at his father-to-be's hands. "But I know just the things to take to raise the money."

Vianne went along to keep herself from judging him, but she began to worry about his motives before they even left their apartment. He took so long getting ready, and sure enough, he came out of the bedroom with his bird mask on.

There were spring blossoms, a clear cobalt sky, a fresh-washed cloudburst, lots of birds. At the end of one alley, two boys were doing skateboard jumps using a sheet of plywood they'd set on blocks. The plywood made a whacking, echoey sound each time they hit it, and the boy watching shouted, "Get a *grip*."

Garnet guided Vianne around them. He had just remembered seeing her brother out in Burnaby. It was at a Shell station. "He looked the same as he did in those photographs you showed me. A bit older."

"He must be just out of prison," Vianne said. "He knows how to rig the pumps."

"No, he paid. And there was a woman with him. And a baby. In one of those car seats." There was an edge to Garnet's voice, a whine, and it excited the crows overhead.

"A baby!" Vianne said. "He must have got her pregnant that time she took the bus down from Prince Rupert. She was his pen pal in prison."

"Vianne. I talked with them at *Christmas*. They've lived in a duplex in *Aldergrove* for the past five *years*. His girlfriend's name is *Denise*."

"Sure, Garn." Vianne grinned. "Jeez, I wish you'd take off your mask. I can't tell what you're thinking."

"I'm thinking about your *brother*," Garnet said. "And I need the mask for the metal. I told you. I'll take it off later."

"Why not now? You don't need it right now. It's like you're not there." Vianne grabbed Garnet's arm to stop him. The alley was white with magnolia petals. "I want you to be there for me," she said.

"I'll be there for you. I will." Garnet snapped a blossom from an overhanging branch. "My sweet Vianne," he said. He gave her the blossom and then pulled her into a weedy yard of an older house. He paused by the garage, listening, and then took her hand up the back stairs past an old couch and through the wide open door of the kitchen. "They think the open door fakes out burglars," he whispered.

Inside the kitchen he pretended to be listening, but Vianne knew he was checking out the toaster, and — could it be? — a golden serving tray hanging on the wall. It was laminated with a snow scene of the Tower of London. The tray was *plastic*. Make him stop, she prayed. Please make him stop.

Garnet was reaching for the tray when they heard steps and the sound of the front door being unlocked. There was just time to drop under the table. The man hung up his coat and went upstairs, but the woman headed for the kitchen. She got a knife and went to the freezer. "Sarah Lee," Vianne mouthed. Garnet frowned, and Vianne gestured to forget it, she would tell him later. The woman stood over the sink, stabbing at the brownies. The sides of her raincoat dragged on the floor. Chunks of brownie and icing flew out and she used her free hand to scoop them into her mouth. It was when she dropped on her knees to gather the fallen pieces that she saw Vianne and Garnet. Her eyes were overly bright, as if she needed an afternoon nap.

"I have an aunt who binged like you," Vianne said to the woman. "Her husband put a lock on the fridge. He got it in writing that she agreed. She copied the key, though, and one night she was ready to hack up the Sarah Lee and there was nothing but snow peas, so she went to the 7-Eleven and asked the kid to bring her some frozen brownies. He said they were at the back, in the freezer, and so she took out her knife and pointed it at him and told him to move. The kid just laughed. You can imagine how mad she was."

The woman rubbed at her white kneecaps. Vianne took a breath to continue and got pinched in the leg. "I don't usually talk about her, but I wanted to let you know you're not alone. Jesus, would you *stop*?" She could not pry Garnet's fingers from her thigh.

The woman shook the crumbs from the pocket of her coat. A lipstick and some change rolled across the linoleum. Vianne reached to help, but Garnet clamped down again on her leg. It was like having her blood let. "Let GO," she hissed. "And why don't you take off that fucking mask?" The worst was feeling that her dirty look was not reaching him through it.

There was the sound of a toilet being flushed upstairs. The woman pulled the icing off the tip of the blade with her teeth while the tank filled. Then she nodded to the door. "Just get out before he comes down," she said.

They were two blocks away before they stopped running. Garnet had to adjust his mask.

"Just take it off. TAKE IT OFF!" Vianne was clawing at it now, and Garnet grabbed her wrists. The boys skateboarded over.

"I'll take it off. Just stop screaming, okay? Vianne? I'm going to let go of your hands now. Don't scream, okay?"

"Take it off or I'll start."

"But . . . "

"Take it off or I'll scream."

"You in a play?" asked one of the boys. He was soft-looking, the kind of boy who said stupid things to make his friends laugh.

"No, he's a *real bird*," said the other. The arrogant kind. He probably wasn't older, but he looked it. Vianne told them to piss off. They made long O's with their mouths.

Garnet lifted the mask. Under it he had been sweating, and Vianne reached up to touch his flattened curls. She kissed him on the mouth.

"I'll have to put it back on, though," he said.

"I know." Vianne rested her chin on his shoulder, and imagined, briefly, that the gentle pressure was a contraption of torture clamping her jaws shut. Then she made a few scary and psycho faces and finally just smiled at the boys, who had stopped halfway down the alley and turned, shamelessly, to watch.

THE LAST FERRY

It was an odd, muffled sound, mechanical yet unsteady, like the bell and spring of an old Olivetti releasing its carriage at startling moments or every time you struck a certain key. The sound grew louder as she approached the terminal.

Across the river the mountains had fallen behind heavy cloud, and even the nearest trees were pale, their trunks silver with disease. It was early November and mild, but the leaves had fallen and the birds were gone. There was nothing at all to flutter.

Perhaps the last scheduled ferry had been cancelled; the lot was empty and the ticket booth appeared to be closed. Then she saw movement. Deep in the ferry walked an erratic figure carrying a light.

Pearl had come to see a doctor, she had come through dark rain and traffic and got lost. She would ask the ferryman for directions.

When she reached the ramp he was gone, and she waited with the heater blowing against her nylons. Her windshield wipers gave the dark scene life, and she prayed in time with them: "God watch over us as we in our nightmares sob, for I in my nightmare dreamed that I did kill, that I would kill again."

Then through the gloom the ferryman appeared, moving across her vision with each sweep of her wipers. When he came into the path of her headlights she saw that he was walking quite steadily; only his flashlight waved like a drunken impulse. He was about to disappear into the darkness again when she honked.

He turned, and his flashlight found her car and fixed it. He made an ambiguous sweeping gesture of invitation, then resumed his course. She started her car and drove in first gear toward his bobbing light. Before she pulled up beside him she swallowed her gum. An old reflex, even though she knew teachers chewed gum and fathers did not always provide.

He waved her into one of the lanes and shrugged to show it didn't matter which one. He smiled as if he had a toothache. Already it was impossible to tell him she wasn't trying to board the ferry. Many of the chronically sick have faith in magical coincidences.

The last one had changed Pearl's life. It was one morning in early October, and many of the people waiting at the bus loop hadn't done up their jackets. She stood outside the shelter, chewing at the inside of her mouth while she looked the people over — one had worn the same pair of jeans for days; another seemed unusually cheerful. Suddenly she saw a man her father's age, a man who had her father's pink cheeks and weathered throat. She hadn't seen him for years, but in an instant she was sick with rage. Murderous rage, and then, abruptly, the urge to kill herself.

Her bus came. Even a lecherous man, a man of a certain age and stiffness of neck, needs to ride the bus, needs a job. Needs love and understanding and the company of his daughter, she told herself. She fantasized how she would carry out her suicide. Surely not with razors or with pills, and she had no gun. The urge was as ordinary as a gas gauge light coming on, a simple problem requiring immediate attention.

She had prayed. She was not religious, yet the words came from a part of her: "I have lost something God gave me. God save me," she prayed, "my air is so thin."

She did not kill herself, but went instead to see a doctor. She spent all of October and most of November seeing doctors, and not one of them gave her drugs, but this last one did give her a referral, he wrote "Ferry Terminal" on a pharmaceutical note-pad.

It was a relief to drive far across the city with her referral; her adolescent desire to commit suicide had long diffused, and now she worried she would not be able to keep her job. Her telephone receiver had grown greasy with use. "Not next week," she told the receptionists at one nearby office and lab after another. "Today."

For this referral, the doctor had assured her, there was no need to make an appointment. She went straight from work the next day. Traffic stopped before the bridge; it was raining, perhaps there had been a stall. Why was it that so often when you were stalled in the rain or hunting through a file folder for an old receipt you felt sudden waves of blood, warmly rejected, waves no napkin could have held? How was it that so much of the tension in your adult life could come from not knowing how much blood there was?

The ferryman was still waving her on, and as she locked her car she saw movement ahead and walked toward it. (Chicks walk toward the first moving figure they see.) There seemed to be a line of figures in the shadows. As she walked through the damp darkness she listened to the mechanical bell, the Olivetti releasing its carriage again and again.

The figures were indeed in a line-up, some of them crouching, others stretching with their hands held high. When she grew close she saw the last one was naked. Indeed, she could see no further than the half-dozen before him, and they too were naked. They appeared to be huddling on a narrow ramp covered with straw; beside them a conveyor belt jerked by with quiet but insistent anarchy. This was the old Olivetti, and when the bell rang the belt moved ahead.

There was something warm and familiar about the line-up, or perhaps Pearl had been feeling terribly cold. As she took her place behind the naked man, she felt a wave of steam so hot it took her breath away. Seconds after she had recovered there was another wave, and another, and finally there was nothing for it but to pull off her clothes, though she knew if the waves of steam were to stop she would freeze.

She was a part of things, now.

Through the steam she heard coughing, the sorts of coughs she had never had to fear; she thought of tuberculosis and smallpox, influenza and diphtheria, and from each one she felt a warm, threatening breath bathe her naked body. They made child's play of her own complaints of twitching muscles, insomnia, dizziness and sudden internal pains — her surrogate-suicide symptoms.

The coughing directly ahead became irritating and she fantasized about clean air ahead lower down, closer to the river. Then she saw that the overhead pulley system was designed to lower the whole line down, on an angle, so only the front half would be submerged.

It would make sense to lower the front end first; surely it was a kind of natural law. But if the front end went down, the rear would have to be lifted still higher into the cold; should she safeguard the clothes that lay beside her gathering dampness?

Thinking this over as she stood in line was like being in grade school, comforting and frightening, the possibility of being right and a bit wrong always with her. At last the ferryman came by, and she called out, "Sir!" and asked him how things were supposed to work. Had each person been summoned to this ferry? Why were they naked and standing in line?

"You'll move up when it's your turn," he said. And then, as if he wanted to soften it, "Usually a lot go out on the weekend."

Pearl began to smell their diseases and realized that their cowering posture and nakedness were the least offensive of their symptoms. The young man ahead of her, chalk-coloured, smelled of rotting meat, and the leprous woman before him of the worst urinal sprayed with heavy floral scent. Pearl could not imagine how she would last, and her clothes, she saw, were now soaked, and covered with a sort of moulted fur. If only she could faint now with disgust.

The belt beside her had been moving steadily, carrying nothing, but now plates of fresh food appeared, rolling past with each muffled ringing of the bell. Ahead she saw arms reaching out, but Pearl could not move. She studied the different foods and the man ahead of her and tried to guess which plate he would select.

She saw he was a young man — perhaps not yet twenty. Steak and fries? A many-layered sandwich? Astonished, she saw him reach for a dish of sliced cucumbers, and now the smell of vinegar marinade was strong, and all at once she was in her place at a smooth white kitchen table, eating her fifth or sixth slice, the sun coming through the window in a warm bar that did not quite touch the dish of cucumbers. The dish was Mel-Mac, and moments earlier her mother had wiped it at the dish rack. It was blueish in colour, light but solid, nothing like the sky or any other blue she could think of. Beside her was her glass of chocolate-flavoured eggnog, untouched, because something about it, the smells mixed together, perhaps, always made her throw up. Her teacher had been sick in the morning and she wondered if she would be sick again in the afternoon or if she would return; with the substitute no one had been allowed to work on the space mural, and the substitute did not know how to do music.

She considered not breathing through her nose while she drank the eggnog. It was nutritious and her mother would be angry if she didn't drink it. But for the moment her mother's back was turned, she was wiping the cutlery, and there was something savage about the way she let each wiped utensil crash into its tray. Pearl had an inspiration. The bathroom door was open; the sunlight danced on the sink. She wouldn't use the sink, the eggnog would leave a scum. She stood, suspended in her excitement, and then she heard her father's steps on the back stairs. The screen door snapped, and then he appeared in the doorway, surrounded by a cloud of frozen air and sunshine.

Pearl hadn't given him a thought since he left the breakfast table, when she saw her mother tilt her face up from spooning out porridge to kiss him goodbye. Now he was breathing all over the room, infecting it. Everywhere Pearl looked, there he was, still smelling faintly of aftershave and hair tonic.

She slid back into her place.

She waited until he was seated and served. She waited until he had taken several spoonfuls of his soup, buttering slices of bread and eating them in wide, wasteful bites.

She raised the glass to her lips, then brought it down again. "May I please be excused?" she finally whispered.

But her father said, "Drink your eggnog, it's delicious," and his anger vibrated all the way to the middle of the night. Then Pearl knew she was causing the bloody and terrible silence of her mother's beating, that her mother's bruises and damaged hearing were not sufficient. She knew she would have to offer herself up to her father in payment.

This memory faded and the conveyor belt came back into focus. Pearl watched tantalizing art supplies go by, neat and bright in their unopened boxes. Here and there were ordinary school supplies like the ones she had used as a child, clean and appealing. Even the stacked pink erasers needed affection, asked to be chosen.

Pearl pressed her lips together and the old Olivetti went "ping" and carried them on.

There was an interval when nothing came by. Pearl's body was coated with sweat; her scalp began to itch. By a wonderful coincidence the next items were pints of beer, a steady line of them, bubbling and cool-looking in their frosted glasses. The boy ahead took one and drank long, and Pearl needed no better advertisement. She too took a glass, and drank until the rising tang of bubbles stopped her.

Immediately she felt a wave of dust. She sat on an old flight of stairs looking across at the other stairs and fire escapes on a street she had lived on in Montreal, her first big city. With her was Luc, wearing his suede-fringed jacket. Luc drank from the brown bottle and then, laughing, handed it to her. She felt her full breasts, the nipples hard under her second-hand sweater. Although it was May, it was still too chilly to sit on the front steps without a coat.

The snow had melted all at once, and she and her roommate dragged the rug outside. Her roommate beat it with her hands with the strength that came from kelp and liver supplements and from being American. Pearl banged the broom against it, awkwardly.

She felt the dirty breeze lift her bangs: damp but still blonde as a password. Not such a bad memory! But as she sat, she saw her mother take this photograph from the letter, and with small, sharp hospital scissors cut Luc off. And she remembered herself, underneath him, waiting for him to stop his proud pumping. She had a longing but it wasn't to bury her face in his flat brown hair, or to kiss his lips — lips that disappeared when he smiled. Then she saw her next boyfriend. Perhaps the longing was for him? Her prince.

She shut her eyes but he continued to shuffle toward her, bent on his apology. Frantic to stop the memory, she reached to touch the coughing, naked boy ahead. His flesh was real flesh, and the instant her fingers made contact she smelled coconut and heard the roaring surf.

They lay, still naked, beside one another on the hot white sand. She saw that the boy's stomach and thighs were covered with open sores, and when she sensed he was about to roll over, turn to her, she groaned aloud. Perhaps this time she was allowed to faint, because it seemed a screen flew up instantly between them, and at her fingertips was an electronic console.

Select: Season/Weather was lit up, and instantly she relaxed into this soothing binary task. Ahead she could make out the boy's screen — he was alone now on his tropical beach — and she saw that others further ahead in the line-up were involved in different landscapes. Pearl selected *Spring, Warm and Overcast*, and for *Actors' Average Age* she chose *12-18*.

She pressed *Go* and smelled a wave of cypress-scented air. She was standing on her ten-speed on a suburban crescent, leaning over the handlebars and feeling the air on her back where her T-shirt slid up from her jeans. She watched her younger self turn to Joy Sanders. (Joy Sandwich, the boys called her, because she was thin, but there was sex in this nickname, and everyone worshipped Joy's long bones, her long black hair.) Pearl turned up the *Volume* and heard shouting from their friend Irene Sawatsky's house. Irene was getting permission to cycle to the mall.

Then Pearl saw another control: *Identification*. She turned the dial to *Closer* and was immediately filled with a restlessness she hadn't felt for years. Now she was leaning against jewellery counters, now prowling through the lingerie and sweaters and shoes and make-up, ducking past the mentally retarded security guard, and then, oddly, now she saw her boyfriend's ex-girlfriend — the one who had once declared at a dance that Pearl wasn't dressed well enough to get in. Through all these images she worried she would not be able to keep up with Irene and Joy on the hills. Irene was fat but strong and Joy would dare anything if Irene wanted her to.

On her own, Pearl avoided hills. It was possible to take a route all the way to Poco with no hills, but the mall was further. You chose between the long hill the Port Moody way, or killer hills going past the asylum.

Irene and Joy had already stolen albums at the mall, and Irene had stolen a knee-length leather coat and modelled it outside the café on Friday night, her pretty lips frozen in a smile.

Pearl felt the ferryman's whisky breath before she turned from the video. He reached across her and turned down the volume. "That mall," he was saying. "Was it up-scale?" He peered into the landscape he had silenced: three long-haired girls cycling toward a river, preparing to cross the bridge single file.

There was something about the ferryman that made her feel sick, the sickness burrowing through her insides and wanting to come up her throat. He turned *Identification* to *Further* and Pearl caught her breath. "It was a suburban mall — families . . . kids . . . "

The ferryman nodded. "We didn't have malls when I was a boy," he said. He paused. "You're here to see the doctor?"

"Is there one? Yes."

"We have to run a check on you first," the ferryman said, and then, with the same grim smile, he turned *Identification* back to *Closer* and walked on, his flashlight bobbing from one landscaped screen to the next.

Pearl had never stolen. In stores she looked for what the popular girls were wearing, and sometimes there was the money to buy a top. Today she knew she was following Joy, whose parents had lots of money and who stole all the time. She was going to see how it was done. But now Joy had disappeared, leaving Pearl in the Young Ingenue section with her bra hook digging into her back, the sweat from cycling having brought out her new allergy to metal. She couldn't reach behind to adjust the flap under the hooks because the saleswoman was already watching her.

Before her were mohair sweaters, each shade filling a cubby of glass and metal tubing. The sweaters were soft-looking, like pastel hamsters. She touched a pink one, felt the saleswoman watching her, and picked it up. Then she took a cream one and the blue one and then a silver one, and a second silver one, quickly, as if such a wide range of colours might obscure the facts.

They were all tight around the neck. The silver one would look good on Irene. She could see Irene's eyes turning misty violet inside her black eyeliner, her sun-bleached hair flat over one cheek. But on Pearl the sweater looked plain grey, and her eyes were as usual, no, worse than the way she was used to seeing them in the bathroom mirror. "I have never stolen," she thought. She pulled her navy sweatshirt over the grey sweater and took her time browsing through a rack of blouses before she left the store.

Joy and Irene were eating hot dogs. "But we'll wait," Irene said cheerfully, with a sparkling hint of menace. Pearl was too jumpy to know if she herself was hungry, but she bought a plain hot dog and ate it quickly, sitting with Joy and Irene on the imitation wood benches. Outside, the warm grey sky made her sleepy, and under her sweatshirt the mohair began to itch at the back of her neck. Her legs were tight from the ride in. I will never do this again, she was thinking, but already Joy and Irene were talking about coming back the next Saturday.

Pearl remembered school a few years earlier: she had got a low mark on a science quiz and so could finally enter the club where you had to have bad marks, C or C- at best, but when she enquired, the standards had changed; now you needed a D to get in.

It began to rain as she passed the mental institution, and Pearl speculated about the extra calories this would make her burn. She was far behind Joy and Irene, but they were waiting at the turn-off.

"Did you get anything? You took so long, we thought you got caught."

Pearl pulled out a bit of grey mohair fluff. "It's like wearing a cat around your neck," she said.

The screen went dark, and the ferryman was beside her again. "That's not why you're here," he said roughly. "You were a *kid*. We didn't have malls," he said again. "We sat on the porch and if we had a nickel we bought a big bottle of Coke."

He was still talking when she heard the first meows. She loved cats and right away she was looking for kittens. A homeless mother cat might like it down here — there must be mice or rats. The ferryman turned away. On impulse she reached out, touched a bit of his orange jacket. "Let's say you belong to a group of unloveable people," she began.

But the ferryman said he had to move on. He left Pearl with her thoughts: if you belong to a group of unloveable people, grown up now, fatter and even more unhappy than when you were sixteen, nevertheless you must not commit suicide, your simpering lips must keep admitting you could get your hair done at an expensive salon, or for God's sake buy some cut flowers.

She was crying by the time she understood to whom this particular voice was addressed: it was to her mother. Why did you stay with a man who did not speak for months and years except in rage, a man whose movements were random and scarcely performed? It was the voice of women writing in their journals to complain about their mothers. It was her own voice.

She managed to stop the ferryman on his way back.

"And the worst for them was they had me," she told him, "a shrinking brat. Shouldn't I have hurled myself out the window?"

The ferryman looked uncomfortable. "You might have written them some nice poems," he said. He was trying to remove a speck from his eye.

"Then I must be here because of my abortion," Pearl said boldly.

The ferryman looked blank, and only with his own voice seemed to regain his stride. "Abortion became illegal only in the nineteenth century," he said. "Efforts to legalize abortion have increased in response to population increases, pressure from women's rights movements, and a high maternal death rate from illegal abortions. Opponents continue to press for prohibition, but no one gets sent here for having abortions." He started to go. But Pearl held him back. She needed to talk about her abortion.

"We were a couple new to our bodies' fire," she began, "our young-thorned bodies dry with thirst appearing, disappearing through the night." The ferryman looked sullen. "He always wanted toast," Pearl continued. "I would have made him a real breakfast but he wanted me to leave so he could get to work."

The ferryman took a paperback from his pocket and, bleary-eyed, found his page.

"There was no plan for it: *abort* meant to miscarry, disappear, off, away, plus to arise, appear, come into being. I would not have enough to offer this baby. No father. Worse, a father who doesn't want to be a father. Who does not love the mother. And I, my little baby, I shook on my two feet, ever the unready." Pearl stared at the console, and its dark dissolved into a pork chop sizzling under a low ceiling, under a white plastic spatula melted in one corner.

There was no God for her. Nothing now was right. O Prince are those your lips? She saw them pink and swollen. There were so many pink erotic things, and some ended in babies. Kettle on. Face washed. This baby would die. Nothing now was right, not the green colour they had painted the walls. Mornings were at least more practical.

It was the day after the day he took her urine in. He got positive results of course. He told her he thought all day about keeping it, but he got so scared, felt so useless. "You're so right for me and I'm all wrong for you," he said, and told her he had lain on the floor and cried. And staring at his weak face Pearl decided there was nothing to live for except other people's children after she murdered her own.

"I knew I would go mad," she wanted to tell the ferryman. But he was up ahead now, speaking with someone with more seniority.

At the time she had considered jumping on a plane for England, where she had a friend. There she'd be, in England.

She was alone and without God.

She walked into the clinic, the modern Church of Referral. She learned that her permanent would be relaxed from the anaesthetic. At twenty-two, her counsellor had already had two abortions and would have another. Large canvasses of acrylic female genitalia covered the walls.

Pearl did not want to be sold a code of conduct, was not doing this for women; she just didn't have the good fortune to swell with her baby and croon. Perhaps she didn't deserve it.

"You're being pressured to keep it," said the girl. "But don't give up." She gave Pearl a referral.

Pearl found that when you are waiting for an abortion nothing happens. There is nothing to tell. She phoned nobody and wrote nothing and did not pick blackberries, no matter how many she saw. Afterward, she imagined the sheets dropped into boiling bleach, her own bloodstains thin and dull. Her thoughts returned, whistling past steel carts through the thickly painted hospital corridors. Leaving no traces no birds no singing anywhere.

"No, it was negative," she told her Catholic co-worker whose boyfriend was always offering, drunk at least, to marry her. "Probably it was stress."

What they did was bring the pregnancy to a premature or a fruitless termination. In morphology spines are aborted branches. We have morphologically sinned, you with your male breasts aborted teats, me with my empty result.

The practice of abortion was one to which few persons in antiquity attached deep feelings. Deep feelings of condemnation, failure of aim or promise, the empty result of any action, in other words our whole relationship, thought Pearl, each time she saw a baby, heard of another abortion.

The empty result was that she never tired of the empty result.

In the recovery room she cried herself out of the anaesthetic. "If you are the doctor! If you can hear me! Please!" She in her nightmare learned that she had killed, would kill again. And was given orange juice in the name of the dead.

The cab driver could smell blood. He drove many women home, refusing to kill them though their despair made them beg.

Later, in her room, on her own again, then in another relationship, then out again, and then, and after that, the story always ends. There is nothing anyone can do.

A woman can miscarry without knowing she has conceived. Something mechanical out of control, the bell and spring of an old Olivetti releasing its carriage forever. The woman could be stirring noodles, or be stalled on a bridge, or hunting through a jammed file for some old receipt. At any time a woman may feel a rejection of blood. She must always scrub the streaks from her panties, scrub out the runes of waves no napkin could hold. Scrub and rinse until her fingers are ice and the water clears.

But you chose to miscarry! You chose to abort! Pay and pay the price! There in the line-up with the festering boy before her she prayed: "God I have miscarried something God-given, something God gave me, God save me, my air is so thin. The leaves do not flutter, the spruce does not complain. God watch over as we in our nightmares sob, as we in our nightmares learn."

The boy ahead of her stank. "These unlovely people," she

told the ferryman, when he returned, "are people whose jeans have not been washed."

"They can take them off," said the ferryman, ignoring, as she had, that the entire line-up was naked.

She was still praying, ". . . as we in our nightmares learn that we have killed and must kill again."

"You were *kids*. You were a couple of young people," the ferryman said.

"New to our bodies' fire," she agreed, nodding, surprised he remembered anything she had told him.

He was shaking his head. "It wasn't the abortion that got you here, it's the living ones you abandoned," he said.

Then she remembered the cats.

"No one comes in for abortion," the ferryman added. "It's things they've forgotten, things they didn't feel bad about."

Now she heard the meowing. It was leaving the cats. "I have been allergic to cats for years," she explained. But now she could see the cats she had left behind. After hatching, she told the ferryman, chicks go toward the first moving object they see. Did she bond with the cats or did they bond with her? Even now when she saw a cat on the street trotting through the mush of autumn leaves she called to it; she knew them all.

The ferryman listened. "So you left them with your father. You ran away, but you left your cats with him. You knew he would get rid of them."

"I couldn't stay with my father," Pearl said.

"You didn't want to?"

Sometimes you want to tell the truth so badly you would give up pleasure, you would give up all sensation. But all around her were stinking bodies, and what was the truth if you didn't know it?

The water below was violet covered with yellow oil. She wanted to be dead. Why couldn't she stay with her father? Because her father was crazy. Why couldn't she just be allowed to die instead of remembering? Her father fooled people — even now she needed multiple opinions, could not trust her own. His effect on her. He was inside her now, out of control. If she killed him she was the one who would die. She didn't want to think. She had a headache. She despised herself and wanted to die. "We don't learn from our mistakes," she told the ferryman, her mouth turned down with disappointment. "There's no reason to stay alive."

"Most people would have done the same thing," the ferryman said. "They would have left the cats." But his objection was mild; it too was part of his job. He showed her a form requiring her signature. It was near the end of his shift. He had nothing to live for; all he did was push people over the edge. "You are given one last chance before you sign," he said. He took a manual from his pocket, found the page and read: "Please imagine you are small again. You are in the bathroom. The adult in charge is about to drown the new kittens."

Pearl could hear the mother cat meowing. The kittens, of course, sounded like mice. She saw the mother cat circling around her father's legs. She was about to right the past! Never had she felt so good. But when she grabbed the kitten from her father, she saw it was missing much of its fur, and the soft bald patches were crowded with tiny black balloons.

"Ticks," the ferryman put in, and Pearl thought she might faint. The mother cat appeared with three more infested kittens.

"Are they going to die?"

"Of course. You shouldn't touch them," he said.

"If it's poison I'll be happy," Pearl whispered. But her jaws had come together. She could not reach out; and she could not open her mouth to speak when the ferryman asked if she'd be taking the cats along home.

The ferryman left her for several hours, but by the end she could no longer look at the cats. The boy in front of her was gone, in fact, all the people who had been ahead of her were gone. She was now at the head of the line-up, and below her was the violet water. "Please," she begged the ferryman. She said it through her teeth, because she knew now that he had always been her father. If nothing else, she prayed, let him do his job.

UNTYING ELINOR

At first Sheila thought Ben was alone — he answered the door, sent David off to the store like a rover for the wine, and took Sheila straight to the kitchen. By the arm. He didn't even give her a chance to take off her coat. Sheila wanted to say something. With Ben, she was always wanting to say something, she was always waiting for a break.

"But that's his method," David said about his father. "He'll never give you a break."

And so Sheila took off her own coat and put it over a chair and turned the situation into a joke: "It's so urgent, the salad?" But Ben didn't answer.

Sheila was a leader, not a follower. She knew this from a vocational aptitude test she'd done in third year. For example, her aptitude for an army career was negative eighteen. But she liked David's father. He'd had a hard time in life, and she pretended she didn't mind the way he was now clutching at her arm again.

No wonder David felt guilty. In this family, guilt was as precious and commonplace as salt. Even when Ben wasn't there. For example, in the bathroom, you couldn't help noticing the re-used dental floss strung over the toothbrushes. This was the guilt of poverty, or perhaps the guilt of miserliness.

Ben propelled her to the cupboards and let go of her arm.

"Do you know how to make salad, Shelley?" he asked.

"Sheila. I can make a great dressing," Sheila said.

"Then I hope David finds another girl to make the salad."

Sheila laughed. "At the liquor store?"

"Well," Ben said. "Where did he meet you?"

Sheila kept smiling. Ben's eyes were close-set, and it felt good to be telling the truth. Even if she didn't doubt for a second that she'd be able to deliver a terrific dressing. And all this was just Ben's way. He made everyone laugh. The first time she met him, she raved about him to David. "I know," David said. "Everybody likes Ben when they first meet him."

In those first weeks Sheila and David had spent a lot of time connecting Ben's eccentricities, but David didn't mention his mother. Sheila finally asked about her.

"She works part-time," David said.

"Oh? What does she do?"

"Telephone soliciting. It's kind of embarrassing."

Sheila hadn't asked why. At that point they'd been going out five weeks, and it was still possible that David was The One. All the time in the world; she'd bring it up again later. Now, six months later, David's father frowned at the head of lettuce he'd just taken from the crisper.

"Where did David meet you?" he asked.

Sheila was saved from admitting the truth — that they'd met in a liquor store — by a woman calling from the living room.

"I've decided about my new car, Ben!" the woman cried.

"Decided what?" Ben called back, much less energetically.

"I'm not going to tell him how much I paid for it!"

"Tell who?"

"Mr. Andrews."

Ben walked to the living room doorway; Sheila followed. Someone — Ben? — had planted a chair inches from a small television (which was not turned on), and a woman's hand lifted and dropped back on the armrest.

"I don't think it's any of his business! Do you, Ben?"

"Think what is?"

"How much my new car cost," the woman said. "Every time, he asks. This time, I'm going to be assertive."

"He's just nosey." Ben went back to the wide-open fridge and knelt again at the crisper. Sheila watched him a moment, then went to the woman in the living room. She meant to introduce herself as casually as possible, but when she saw that the woman was tied to the chair with what looked like the very wool with which she was (or had been) knitting a sweater, Sheila froze.

"Don't we have any olives?" Ben called.

"Where are you looking?" Ben's wife called back. Sheila assumed it was Ben's wife. Elinor. That's what David called her.

Elinor smiled up at Sheila.

"I've thought up a good one," Elinor said. "I'll say, 'Mr. Andrews, I've decided that I don't wish to reveal that information.' Is that assertive or is that assertive?"

"It sounds, um, fine," Sheila said. Tied to a rocking chair in front of the TV! Obviously this "tied in" with family stuff — but how? And was it her business? Would it be more her business if she were sure that David was The One? Was this the sort of thing people in crowds ignored because each assumed someone else was calling the police? But there was no one else around! She had to untie Elinor! Obviously! She took a step closer.

"You don't think he'll think I'm hard?" Elinor asked. She was still smiling, and her eyes were the unblinking blue kind that young girls have when they are the smartest in the class.

"No, I . . . " Sheila held out her hands and was about to kneel beside Elinor when Ben came out of the kitchen.

"Take whatever you need from the fridge, Sheila," Ben said. He took her elbow and prodded her back into the kitchen. Then he stood in the doorway like a gateman.

"Two kinds of lettuce, tomatoes, radishes, green pepper . . . I don't know if you like green pepper, Sheila."

"Yes. Yes, I do," Sheila said. She put her hand on a head of iceberg lettuce. What else could she do?

"Green onion, ordinary onion — I think there's a dicer around. Garlic — will you need a garlic press?"

"Oh, not really, I can . . . "

"Let me just get that press." Ben pulled out a drawer, pushed utensils around, slammed the drawer shut, opened another, slammed it shut. "Elinor! Where did you put that garlic press?"

"It's hanging," Elinor said. "It's hanging over beside the knives."

"Hanging!" Ben said in a low voice. He giggled. "The garlic press is hanging." He nudged Sheila with his elbow, even though she was several feet away. She began to consider that he might actually be a crazy man, and without thinking moved a step further away.

Sheila got the cutting board and began to chop radishes. She decided she'd chop three and then excuse herself to use the bathroom and then she'd untie Elinor. She'd chopped three and was about to excuse herself when the doorbell rang. She would chop another radish, and when Ben went to get the door, she'd go untie Elinor.

But Ben didn't move. He kneeled at the crisper, using his right hand to load up his left arm with vegetables. Elinor called from the living room: "Ben? Aren't you going to get that?" and Ben called back, "My hands are full."

"Ben?" Elinor called again.

Ben could easily have put down his armful of lettuce and broccoli and cabbage. Was he planning to put all those things in? What kind of salad was he planning to make?

"I'll get the door," Sheila said. She rinsed her hands, shook them, and wiped them on her jeans. Ben stood with his armful of vegetables, watching her.

"You don't need to," he said coldly.

There were voices in the front hall. Sheila heard Elinor's.

"I'm afraid we don't," Elinor said. "We have enough to last months as it is." Whoever was at the door said something, and then Elinor said, "But I wouldn't want to give them to the neighbour children." The person at the door had another chance, and then Elinor said, "No, really. I just don't want any." Sheila heard the door close. Elinor appeared in the kitchen doorway. Her cheeks were flushed.

"They can be such pests," she said.

"Who?" Ben asked.

"Those salesmen. You know."

"I don't know. I wasn't there."

"Oh, Ben. You're not putting all that in the salad."

"All what?" Ben said.

"Well. Cauliflower with cabbage? Look there. Is that mould?"

"What?"

Elinor and Ben's heads came together over a green pepper. Twenty-five years they'd been married. That was the problem, David said: his father had married too young. "What about your mother? If she's five years younger, she must have been a teenager." That's what Sheila wanted to say. But that was when Sheila and David had been going out for only a few months. The stage when confessions were never challenged. Sheila stepped out of the intimate scene into the living room. She picked up Elinor's knitting, and was trying to figure out how Elinor had untied herself when Ben came up behind her.

"Giving up already, Shelley?" he asked. He guided her back into the kitchen. Elinor had gone out the other way. Sheila heard the toilet flush. She picked up the bread knife she'd been using to chop radishes and looked around for something else to do. She was distracted with waiting for Elinor to come back. "There's no particular order you have to follow," Ben said. "Onions, carrots, broccoli — broccoli, onions, carrots! Hang loose a little, Shelley." He left the room. Sheila cut herself, and felt a mild stinging. She watched the blood diffuse on her wet finger.

David would be back soon. Where had he gone for wine? There was a liquor store a few blocks away. Maybe he'd gone for cranberries. It was Thanksgiving, but there was no turkey, no ham, no mention, in fact, of its being a holiday. But she'd never seen David at Thanksgiving before — perhaps he always went out to buy cranberries. Perhaps he just liked them. Perhaps he preferred the frozen ones — they were often hard to find.

"I'll stay here," she'd said. "I'd like to spend some time alone with your father." Forty dollars worth of wine, Ben had asked for. David had stood a long time, and Sheila guessed he was waiting for his father to give him some money. But Ben didn't give him any. Forty dollars was a lot for one dinner, and if Ben hadn't been right there Sheila would have asked David if it was for a carton or what, because if it was for some 1973 Beaujolais he could count her out. No, she wouldn't have said anything to David; she hadn't known him long enough. She glanced through the door to the living room. She couldn't be sure, but it looked like Elinor was tied up again. Fine, she thought, stay tied up. David couldn't be much longer.

She rummaged through the pile of vegetables on the counter. Where was the lettuce? Radishes, green onions, carrots, parsley, cauliflower, green cabbage, red cabbage, green pepper, red pepper, mushrooms, chives; but no lettuce.

"What are you looking for?"

"Lettuce."

"Iceberg lettuce?"

"Any kind."

Ben inclined his head, as if to let the defiant tone of Sheila's words go out into the universe.

"It's mouldy. You'll have to improvise," he said. "Or are you one of these people who have to go by the rules?"

Sheila felt the anger in her stomach, felt it making its way up her chest. It was at her throat when Ben moved so close she could smell garlic. "But it's not just that he's obnoxious," she told herself. "And it's not just the way he treats his wife or the way he treats me." In her hand was the bread knife, and she fought with herself to keep from lifting it. She watched her hand rise, the knife tip pointing down a little, inches from Ben's cotton golf shirt.

"Just teasing." Ben pushed at the air between them with the palms of his hands. "The lettuce is already out," he said. "Right in front of you."

Sheila whirled around. So it was. "Oh, I see it," she said. Her anger was frozen now, but she knew she'd have to monitor her urge to stab the lettuce. Ben began to transfer the load of vegetables from beside the fridge to the counter by the sink, where Sheila was stationed. She pulled apart the leaves. When she'd finished washing them she was going to go untie Elinor — if Elinor was tied up. She wasn't going to excuse herself in any way; she was going to walk into the living room and do it. Then Ben left the room, and Sheila heard him talking with Elinor. Sheila opened the fridge, looked for mustard, or oil, or vinegar.

"What do you need now? Tomatoes are right there. Celery's out. That's horseradish. Is it horseradish you're looking for?"

"No. Mustard."

"Mustard? You want to put mustard in the salad?" Ben began to cackle.

"It's for the dressing."

"Oh," Ben said. He nodded a series of long, long nods. He kept nodding and Sheila kept staring at him and finally she turned and walked into the living room. Yup: Elinor was tied up tight. Gagged, now, too, with a foolish cotton bandanna. Sheila felt a wave of nausea and took a breath. The knife. That's what she needed. Ben was standing in the doorway. She pushed by him, got the knife, and pushed by him again. But he followed her to Elinor's chair and stood over her as she untied the bandanna. The knot was loose, inexpertly tied, and hung down by one side of Elinor's face. She began to saw through the strands of wool. She could see Ben's fingers trembling beside her and after a moment she turned to him.

"Are you crazy, what are you doing?" Ben said.

Sheila twirled the knife gently, watched it catch light up and down the blade, and when she looked up she saw all sorts of things reflected in Ben's eyes: the fridge, the ceiling light, the fireplace. Her own frightened face.

"She doesn't mean any harm, Ben," Elinor said.

"I don't know," Ben said. "She's acting pretty wild. We still don't know where David met her."

"Oh, Ben." Elinor moved her hand along the armrest, and Ben covered it for a moment with his own, and gave her a stagy look of fortitude and suffering.

Sheila looked down at the knife and then at Ben. "Do you think I'm crazy?" she asked him.

"Well, you're acting crazy. I don't know if you act this way all the time. Do you?"

"I think the question is whether you act this way all the time."

"What way? You women! You're always so imprecise!"

That's when Sheila would have thrown the knife across the room into the wall. It would have made an open, dead sound, and bounced to the floor along with nicked bits of chalky Gyproc. But Sheila didn't throw the knife; she dropped it and walked out. She met David in the hall. He saw her face and waited. "Your father's a real nutcase," Sheila said. "Tying your mother up like that."

"I know," David said. "It's a madhouse."

Sheila pushed the elevator call button and it lit up. There was a testy silence.

"So . . . you're going?" David said.

"I'm going."

"You know, the thing is, my mother likes being tied up," David said. He put his bag of wine on his other hip.

"She likes being tied up," Sheila said. "You know that? You've asked her?"

"Well. You know how you just know some things?"

They turned at the same time to see Ben, wearing an old car coat and followed by Elinor, who was fishing in her purse, going through one compartment after another. "I just can't find them, Ben," Elinor said.

"Nobody's going to break in," Ben said, winking at Sheila. He took Elinor's arm and pulled her to the elevator. "We'll just go out for dinner," he said. "Though I didn't think there'd be such a fuss over a salad." He pushed the elevator button, and then, perhaps because it didn't become extra-bright, he pushed it again. Sheila nudged David, and then pinched his arm, but when he did look at her, his lips were pressed together, and she turned away.

On the street, Ben said, "We might as well walk to that pizza place Elinor likes." David was shivering, eyeing the traffic; Elinor looked pleased, but a little puzzled. Sheila stood apart, and when they set out, she dragged behind, and it was such a slow procession that she had time to hear whole, recurring phrases in her thoughts between each step: she'd say goodbye at the corner, at the corner at the latest, and this would keep her from doing a crazy thing, and she knew it was a crazy thing, a crazy thing to want to stay.

THE LAST SUCH CONVERSATION

Diane spent her two years as a volunteer believing it was theft to take people's pictures without their knowledge — zooms of herdsmen or milkmaids taken from a moving vehicle were very wrong. She had taken nothing from the culture without permission, and nothing that she did not need to live: food, cloth to make the clothes she wore, new sandals when her own broke. Now she was about to leave Nigeria; she had in her possession a British Airways ticket for the following day's flight leaving from Kano. The ticket was too long and bulky to fit next to her passport in the flat leather case she wore under her top, and she was carrying it in the money-belt she wore around her waist.

Other volunteers she knew had bought yards of wax print cotton to take home. Leather bags. Carved wooden animals. One teacher had filled several shipping containers with farm and household implements — machetes, brooms, buckets — to show schoolchildren at home how the Nigerians lived. Another had video footage of students killing a poisonous snake at the water tank.

Now, on her last day in the country, Diane wished she too had things to bring home. She wished she hadn't been quite so self-interrogating. It was too late, of course, to take photographs, or to find something wonderful, such as a child's train set made from canned milk tins.

The idea of buying some beautiful wax print cloth or some local indigo tie-dye came to her during her eight-hour taxi journey from her northeastern posting. There was no longer a hostel in Kano for Canadian volunteers, so she had checked into the Durbar Hotel, planning to spend the next day shopping in the old Kano market. In the morning she left her luggage at the hotel and took a town taxi to the market.

It was like sliding down a scorching bank into a thick, cool river as she entered the covered market. She imagined the heat above sizzling up into a vast sky, while slick fingers of rippling darkness played on her shoulders, gently guiding her, as if she were a rat scurrying to make use of the current in her short, insignificant life. She had entered the cloth section, and the pungent odour of indigo was strong. She hoped to spot a place to sit — a stool, a soft-drink crate — somewhere she might enjoy a Fanta and consider which gifts to buy.

First she had to get rid of the tout, a tall, skinny man who seemed to have been waiting for her as she stepped out of the taxi. He followed at a discreet distance, murmuring suggestions as she turned from one narrow corridor into another. Cloth traders sat in the gloom behind long, fat bolts of brilliant prints. "Dutch Wax, Madam, very cost," said the tout. "But not cost with me. Customer, let me show you, customer. Madam, I am carrying your loads." But Diane had arrived at just the wrong moment. Most of the Muslim cloth traders were leaving their kiosks to go to prayers, and she had only a short time to examine some of the crisp, heavy cotton before the traders spread sheets over their cloth and fastened the zinc shutters of their stalls.

She turned another corner and was in the leather goods section.

"Leather, buy leather," the tout encouraged. "Continue straight, straight." The leather traders were also leaving for prayers. The corridors were suddenly crowded with men carrying their teakettles for ablutions.

But the tout held his position. Diane wanted to tell him he was wasting his time. She even thought of ducking into an empty stall to hide. But she could never be sure that an empty stall *was* empty; a trader might have unrolled his prayer mat in that dark space behind the display. She had to put up with him.

When she first got out of the taxi she had seen the tall, foolish-looking youth wearing an orange net T-shirt and with a row of black rubber gasket-rings pushed high into the muscle of his forearm. Now he looked even thinner, and older, and in the dark corridors of the market his vanity had been replaced by skill. He was hungry and he needed money. His deep voice, striking in such a spindly man, turned wicked.

All at once the corridors were empty and quiet. She wouldn't have a chance of losing him until the traders returned from prayers. She entered a new corridor, recognized an elaborate display of beaded bracelets, and realized she had already walked past it. She turned, crying out as she nearly collided with the man. But he managed to turn at almost the same moment, leaping in a tidy pirouette as if they were magnets and were from time to time flipping poles. He shrank against a wall of leather handbags, allowing her once again to take the lead.

What would stop him from following her all day long? Would she be the one to give up? Would that mean allowing him to carry something and make suggestions, or would it mean abandoning her idea of buying cloth? She might take a casual route back to the entrance of the market and stand there pretending to inspect bicycle hawkers' earrings or cassettes; then, when the first town taxi was available, she might quickly enter it. Losing him. Speeding to the Durbar Hotel, and then, at this time tomorrow, flying all the way to Canada to lose him!

She was somehow back in the cloth section now. The Muslims were returning from prayers, and she recognized a trader whose indigo waxes she had admired when she first entered the market. "You're back!" he cried. "Madam! I'm giving you a reduction!"

Diane glanced behind her. To her amazement, the tout was

walking away. He stood out in his orange shirt among the shuffling corridor of men.

"I'm back," she agreed. "What is your last price for this indigo wax?" She began to bargain. The trader asked her where her husband was — he was in the house, she replied — and told her that her skill speaking Hausa was excellent. The trader beside him straightened his gown and declared that Diane would be his wife. Diane laughed. "You have enough wives already," she said, and they all laughed.

"Come, customer, bring eighty naira — that is my last price," the first trader added casually.

"That is a huge amount. I'll bring you fifty naira. Last."

"Well, then, that's all. There's nothing to be done," the trader said, turning away. Diane had gone the distance of a few stalls when he called her back.

"Bring your money," he said mournfully.

Diane reached to zip open her money-belt. Any one of the women teachers at her school would have held their ground and brought the price down to forty naira. Never mind. She needed a Fanta. She patted the space where her money-belt usually hung and felt nothing but her own stomach. The belt wasn't there.

"*Mallam,*" she cried, gesturing to its absence. "I don't see my money-belt . . . there is no belt. . . . Where is the belt?" She spoke entirely in Hausa, hoping one of the men would offer it up out of the gloom of a stall. A fly was bothering an empty soft drink bottle, banging against it again and again. "Sorry, Madam," said the trader. "Sorry. Next time you'll bring money." He said this last severely, as if he were expecting her to beg to take the cloth on credit.

"No! A thief! *Barawo*!" Diane tried again.

"Yes. *Thief*. Next time, Madam." The trader began to rearrange his bolts of cloth to close for the day.

Two-thirty. At this time the next day she would be in a lineup at the Kano airport. This was not a good time to lose her air ticket. She began to walk back in the direction of the motorpark. She would go back to British Airways. She must hurry, before it closed. They would remember her. They would have a record. Of course, that wouldn't help if there was no power and the computer was down. Or if British Airways closed early on Friday. But why should it? She would give the clerk something for a printout of the passenger list with her name on it. Her copper bracelet. No, that was worthless. Her watch, perhaps.

She was humming a nervous little song as she turned into a new corridor. By moving somewhat diagonally she hoped to reach the motorpark more quickly.

She was now in the plastics section. There was no end to the miraculous pyramids: cups, buckets, basins . . . in some cases traders had somehow built them higher than the stalls themselves. The last arrangement of the corridor promised to be the most spectacular, and she approached it with regret, as she would a favourite exhibit in an art gallery she had no time to admire. She complimented the trader — a large Ibo woman who had to keep shouting at her children to pay attention and be careful as they ran lightly in and out of the remarkable pyramids — and then she saw that the corridor was a dead end.

She asked the woman where the motorpark was, and the woman gestured firmly in two different directions. "I'm going to British Airways," Diane said, hoping her destination would help the woman determine the right motorpark. But the woman shook her head. "Onitsha," the woman explained. Perhaps she was telling Diane where her own home was. "Are there two motorparks?" Diane asked.

The woman clapped her hands. Once again she gestured in one direction and then the other.

Diane thanked her and turned, swallowing the urge to sob. She had been standing and walking for hours. She was thirsty. She followed one of the woman's directions towards a wide, bright corridor. It turned out to be a long one, filled with the whirring of sewing machines. May it reach the motorpark, she prayed, and she believed that over the noise of the machines she began to hear the sounds of motorpark shouting and commotion in the distance ahead.

Finally the darkness ahead grew black, and she knew the corridor was about to turn. The motorpark! Fanta! Never mind about paying. She would plead with the hawker. She was white. Very weak! She had to drink something! She would give *him* the copper bracelet.

She began to hurry, and just before the corner she stumbled and fell. It was a silly thing, but she had twisted her ankle. There were no customers, and she considered lying there in the coolness, but she was far too thirsty to stop thinking of the Fanta. She pulled herself up and hobbled to the corner.

"*Ba hanya*! Madam!" There was no road, the trader was calling. Sure enough, she had come to another dead end.

"*Ga hanya a nan*!" The trader was eager to show her the way out. He seemed to be indicating an exit halfway down the corridor. Had she walked right past it? She leaned a moment against the mud wall, pressing her thumb into the soreness of her ankle. Which was worse, pain or thirst? Thirst. Good body, she muttered. We just have to get to the motorpark.

She walked painfully back past the tailors, greeting some of them simply because it made her progress less tedious. "Greetings, *mai-dinka*," she said, stopping to press and turn her ankle. "How is the tiredness?" And when the tailor asked, she told him her husband was fine. He was in the house.

Now most of the stalls were closed, their shutters loosely padlocked. Clearly the traders had secret escapes. She imagined them tunnelling their way straight out of the market, emerging at the correct side of the motorpark for the VW van that would carry them home with their loads.

She entered another corridor. She wished she hadn't lost the tout. After all, she had no money now — she had nothing to lose by allowing him to lead her back out of the market.

The sharp light at the end of the corridor and the sound of highlife music told her she had arrived at the motorpark, but she heard none of the shouting between drivers and hawkers, and feared she had arrived at an unfamiliar and out-of-the-way entrance. Well then: she would ask the way to British Airways and to the Durbar Hotel. If the Durbar was closer — and she thought it must be — she would walk, and from there telephone British Airways. She was now accustomed to the pain in her ankle, and besides, Kano was the biggest northern city. You were always running into someone you knew. Someone she knew might spot her and offer a lift. She would soon be sitting under a cool fan at the Durbar. It would be easier to think once she'd had a Fanta.

But turning the corner she found herself, not in the motorpark, but in a whole new section of the market concerned with hardware and electrical supplies. She had no idea if the motorpark lay beyond or far behind, but she was relieved to see the Ibo traders. The highlife music was coming from one of the stalls. Inside, and surrounded by towering shelves of cassettes — one of them the revolving type — a young Ibo man was dubbing from a highlife record to a cassette. He sat on his stool with one hand poised over the record player.

Diane waited to ask directions to the motorpark.

"I'm coming," the man said without looking up. Then came the skip, and he caught the needle and instantly replaced it where the record wasn't damaged. Then he snapped his fingers and called out, "Godswill!" A boy's sleepy face appeared around the back curtain. The man told him to bring two Cokes, and the boy ran off. "Very cold," he called after him. The record stopped. He turned it over and made adjustments to the cassette recorder. When the music began again he sat back, then leaned forward to turn it up, presumably for her sake.

"Sit down, please!" he said. He shouted over the music. "From where? US? Canada?"

"Yes — Canada."

"Fantastic. I had one teacher, Miss Hammond. My name is Joseph."

Diane nodded and smiled. Her ankle was throbbing again. "I'm Diane. I've been teaching here, too," was all she could think of to say. It would be rude to bring up the motorpark so soon.

"In Kano?"

"No — near Yola. Gongola State."

Joseph frowned. "Have you been to Onitsha? Owerri? Have you seen Anambra State?"

"Yes," Diane said. "It's great," she added with enthusiasm. The boy was back, holding out an Afri-Cola.

"May I open it?" he asked her.

She drank it straight down. Joseph and Godswill watched her sympathetically. Before she could explain about her money, Joseph announced that, unlike some Hausa traders, he believed in offering refreshment to his customers. Godswill opened the second bottle, remaining by her side to take it as he had the other.

She had nothing to offer them. No money, no stickers . . . no Canadian souvenirs. But now that she was no longer thirsty, she had a clearer perspective. One thing at a time.

"I've lost my money-belt," she began. "My air ticket was in it. For tomorrow's BA flight. And my money. I'm hoping to get to British Airways."

The trader shook his head. "Don't worry, Madam," he said. "I know one man at the airport. He is related to my brother Emmanuel. Godswill!" He spoke at length in Ibo to the boy, giving a complicated sounding list of instructions. "Godswill will go to my brother Emmanuel. Emmanuel is a very rich businessman," he told her. "He will help you, if you agree."

Diane glanced at Godswill. His smile was huge. "May I go, Madam?" he asked.

Diane hesitated. "I was just thinking of going to British Airways to get a duplicate ticket. . . . If you could help me get out of the market . . . "

But Joseph shook his head. "You are injured," he said. "And now you have lost your money. BA will not give you another ticket again."

"Even if they just have to print out a second copy?"

"No, Madam. They will not agree." Joseph stopped his tape and took the needle off the record. It seemed he needed quiet to think. "The best plan is for my brother Emmanuel to intervene at the airport. Yes . . . he has one relative there, although most of those airline workers are Hausa men. Nevertheless my brother is an important businessman. He will get you on that flight." Joseph nodded to Godswill, who was still poised to go.

"All right. It's probably too late to get to BA now anyway. Perhaps he could take me to the Durbar. My luggage is there," Diane said.

"Emmanuel will take you, Madam." Godswill ran off.

From the hotel Diane would make arrangements. She couldn't remember if the Durbar Hotel had a telephone. She would ask the brother. If it didn't, she would ask to go straight to the NET telephone office.

"Madam, my brother will not delay," said Joseph. He listened to a segment of tape, set the needle back on the record in precisely the right place and went on with the dubbing.

"Do you know our music?" he asked. Diane said yes, and pointed to an album cover of one of the musicians she knew.

"Osadebe. He is very, very popular," agreed Joseph.

Diane pulled a stool over to rest her ankle.

Half an hour passed before Godswill returned. By then her ankle had swollen to twice its size, and when she tried to walk darts of pain shot up from her foot.

"My brother is waiting at the entrance with his machine. I will carry you," said the boy. This made them both laugh.

"Of course not. But perhaps I could lean on you," Diane said. Godswill reminded her of one of her first-form students. "Is it far?" she asked. "Or will we be there soon?"

"Yes," said the boy immediately.

They walked on, and each time Diane drew her breath in with the pain the boy cried out in sympathy. "Sorry, Madam!" he said, and although she suspected he was bewildered at her frailty, his words helped her to continue. But when they came to the traders where Diane had bargained for the indigo wax and discovered her money-pouch was gone, she collapsed against a wall.

"Sorry, Madam," said Godswill. "Sorry."

"I can't walk," she said. The wall was luxuriously cool.

Godswill kneeled beside her. "Madam. Let us trek. These Hausa traders . . . " He was uncomfortable in this part of the market, even if the traders were gone.

But Diane couldn't make herself move.

It was then that a most amazing thing happened. Someone knocked on the back wall of the indigo cloth trader's. Godswill opened the shutters and ran in — evidently the trader had no padlock — and pulled the zinc window back. There, backlit by the low evening sun, stood a man in a shirt and blue jeans. Beside him was a Honda 280. The only such motorcycle Diane had seen was a policeman's.

"Good evening," the man called from inside the halo of sun. "Godswill, bring the lady to the first exit." He added something in Ibo. Godswill shouted his agreement and helped Diane fifty feet to an ordinary entrance. How could she have missed it?

"Don't worry, Madam," he said, pulling her the last few feet. "My brother Emmanuel is very rich. Everything will move smoothly. We thank God day and night!"

Godswill stood stiffly as his good-looking brother handed him several five-naira bills. Then he turned back to Diane. "Goodbye, Madam. We thank God!" he said, and ran back into the market.

Diane was left with the brother. The street food vendors were lighting their fires to heat their oil for frying, and these brave lights began to fill the side of the boulevard. Across the rubble-filled field was a paved road, and there was an illusion of moisture in the air, as if there were many trees instead of the one cranky baobab tree beside them. In this country Diane knew how to feel glad for what she had. For the first time she had understood the word *enough*.

"You've hurt yourself," the man remarked. "Are you ready?" He explained that it was too late to find British Airways open, but he could arrange for her to retain her place on the passenger list. Wouldn't she like to go back to her hotel to relax while he took care of it? By the way, he said, his name was Emmanuel, or had Joseph and Godswill already told her? And had they told her how rich he was?

In the glare of the sunlight he could have been joking or he could have been serious. He got on the bike and encouraged her to join him.

"You are American. OR CANADIAN," he shouted, as he made the engine start with a wonderfully unnecessary roar. He radiated a pleasant scent of cologne and hair tonic.

"YES — CANADIAN."

"Ah, CUSO. Don't worry. I know your officer, Mr. Richard. A jolly fellow at a party."

Emmanuel turned to make sure Diane had located the footrests. Diane was not sure she had heard correctly. *Richard*. All the field officers had names like Richard — Richard or Robert. You didn't bother a Richard. Richards were under a great deal of stress. When your salary was withheld you did not go to Richard. One Richard had gone crazy, or something like it. A reaction to the anti-malarial prophylaxis.

They flew over the hard, cracked clay to the trees lining the motorpark. Diane let her cheek graze Emmanuel's billowing shirt.

Emmanuel drove through the dust and the noise, which was muted by the sudden coming of night. There was a satisfying smell of deep-fried fish and yam and beancakes, even at the major landmarks and roundabouts. Emmanuel abruptly turned in at the Durbar Hotel and parked, taking up two spaces.

"Now, something cool," he said, holding the door open.

Diane asked if there was a phone. "There may be," Emmanuel said. "But it surely won't be working." He told her not to worry about her ticket. First they would enjoy a meal, and then he would go directly to the airport to speak to his relative. He found them a table and called for a waiter.

"Have you seen all the states in the federation?" he asked, smiling, already looking bored.

Diane began to name the states and tribes she had visited, but most were in the north, and Emmanuel, who was Ibo, interrupted her.

"These Hausa think they can control the federation," he said darkly. He tried another tack. "What brought you to Nigeria?" he asked. The conversation turned from aid organizations to missionaries to the problems facing Africa and the trouble with Nigeria. By then Emmanuel was holding forth. This was not the conversation Diane would have chosen, and Emmanuel did not appear to be enjoying it either. When the waiter came he looked relieved. He ordered expensive beer and several dishes of meat and plantain and jollof rice.

Diane asked for two Fantas and drank them down. They were cold and highly carbonated. "Ahh," she said. "Emmanuel, I'm so grateful to you for helping me."

"Don't mention it," said Emmanuel. "So! There it is: Nigeria, giant of Africa. Rich in resources, lacking in leadership." His duty done, he began an entertaining story about his university years in the US. The story circled back to his boyhood in Enugu, where in first form he had a Canadian teacher everyone wanted to sleep with. The boys. The staff. All the men in the town. But no was *no* with that lady!

He laughed together with Diane. "And did you refuse admirers on your tour here?" he asked.

Diane nodded. "Not that I wasn't attracted to them." She was leaving now. She could say what she liked.

"Naturally. But there are two types of women." Emmanuel sighed. "I have never paid a woman to sleep with me," he declared after a pause. "What is disturbing you? Is it still your air ticket? Don't worry. My brother will arrange everything. But may I ask one favour."

"Of course." Diane expected a request to send something from abroad. Automobile tires, electronic goods. A washing machine. But Emmanuel's request was none of these.

His friends would be along to join him. "As of now. At any time," he added.

Diane waited. She had spent enough time drinking Fanta with rich men to know that they saw their friends on informal but predictable daily circuits. Obviously the Durbar Hotel was one stop on Emmanuel's route. "Here?" she said helpfully.

Why not? Did she prefer the Central Hotel? That was not a problem. But here was the favour: he wanted her to talk about his house. He would describe it so she would know how everything was. "In my house, do you know how many electrical appliances we have?"

Diane thought a moment. "Two?" she asked.

"Two! Two! We have sixteen," Emmanuel said.

"Are you counting ceiling fans?" Diane asked.

"Of course. Are you offended?" he added, when she looked puzzled.

Then she smiled. She was leaving. This was the last such conversation she would have. She relaxed, and her tone became teasing: "Oh, you want me to pretend to be your girlfriend?" she asked.

"What?" Emmanuel cried. How could she be his girlfriend when they had just met?

Then who did he want her to be?

Now Emmanuel looked confused. Who?

Who! she repeated. A friend of a friend? Perhaps a customer — did he have goods to sell? Perhaps she'd gone to his house to see samples . . . although she had to tell him that to a westerner this would sound suspicious.

Emmanuel nodded. Then who did she want to be? Did she like to pretend to be different people? Such as his girlfriend? He had no quarrel with that. Anyway, he said, given time, and with many similar interests and their mutual love for life, who could say? They might indeed become lovers. Although it was a pity she was leaving the next morning on the BA flight.

"But let me try to understand," Diane said. He wanted her to somehow impress his friends. Was that it?

"Who told you I wanted to impress my friends?" he asked.

"Don't you? Please don't answer the Nigerian way with another question."

Emmanuel smiled. "Do you think I am a vain person?" he asked. The waiter brought plates of meat and yam and jollof rice. Emmanuel pushed them in front of Diane, and she pushed them back into the middle and asked if they could share.

"So, you like the African way," Emmanuel said without enthusiasm. They ate in silence.

Emmanuel ordered more beer and Fanta, and Diane took the chance to ask what it was he wanted her to pretend to have done at his house. To have taken food with him? Read his magazines? Admired his photograph albums?

But now Emmanuel looked irritated. "I don't need any of those things," he said. "I only wish you could see for yourself the way I am living. Not like so many of these northerners, with their mud walls . . . "

The waiter brought chicken pepe soup, and they ate again in silence.

When Emmanuel had finished he washed his hands carefully and drank long from his beer. He was a handsome man, and Diane liked watching him.

Could it be he wanted her to talk about his sixteen appliances?

The waiter was back. "Madam, there is a boy at the gate. They refuse to let him in. He is unkempt. He claims he has something of yours."

It was the tout. When she dropped her bag he had picked it up. Then he could not find her again. Finally he was asking and asking everyone in the market and finally these Ibo traders told him the white woman went with one Ibo man to the Durbar Hotel.

Most of her money was gone. "Madam, everyone was surrounding me, shouting. I don't know if I have replaced all the naira."

"That's all right," Diane said. Once again the tout looked thin and ailing. Diane insisted he take a reward. "A small gift," she said.

Emmanuel sat stiffly throughout the exchange, but as soon as the tout was gone he exploded. "Why did you give money to that man? He is a thief!"

"But I'm so relieved to get my ticket back," Diane said. "It's my last day here. I don't need the money . . . I was going to buy gifts . . . " She shrugged, and felt herself blushing. She was thinking, it doesn't matter. Nothing that I do today matters. I could make love with this man and it wouldn't matter.

"You give him a reward for returning your empty bag . . . *na-wa-o*! In my place, nobody would do such a thing. In my place . . . "

She stopped him. "Emmanuel," she said. "I want to go to my room and rest."

Could he see her to her room? Of course, she said. They passed a pretty young girl dressed up for her night of prostitution. Her gaze lingered on Emmanuel, and in it Diane thought she saw a playfulness.

"She is here every night," Emmanuel said, guessing her thoughts. "Delightful. But as God is my witness, I have never given in to her charms."

The room was not quite as she'd left it: the mattress was bare. There was a pile of folded sheets on the chair.

Emmanuel turned on the fan, opened the window wide to the darkness, and swept the mattress with his hand. He instructed Diane to sit and rest her ankle while he made the bed. He threw each sheet on with an expert snapping sound. There was a catching happiness in his gestures. As she watched him, Diane made a sleepy list: she had her air ticket; she had money to get to the airport; the tout was a scoundrel but could have sold the ticket; she had eaten a good meal; Emmanuel was terribly handsome. It had been a good day. She was ready to sleep.

Then she realized she had no way of making sure she woke up in the morning. Ordinarily she woke at six, but what if she didn't? She had to be at the airport by seven or eight at the latest to check in.

She asked Emmanuel if someone could make sure she was up at six. "I am at your service," Emmanuel said. "I have no engagement. I will sleep now, and stay awake later, while you sleep." He sat in the chair and shut his eyes.

Diane put her head back and was instantly asleep. She woke to a fierce pain in her ankle. She heard Emmanuel breathing in his chair. She wondered if it felt like this to have a *maigardi* — a personal night-watchman. She pulled off her bra and underwear and lay in her wrapper. She directed her thoughts to stop at her knee so she would not feel her ankle.

A second time she awoke to hear Emmanuel snoring. "Emmanuel," she said, reaching to touch his leg at the ankle. From his chair his outstretched leg formed a near-right-angle to hers. "Emmanuel! If I sleep and you sleep, who is going to wake me up?"

"I am awake," he said. "Don't worry."

The next time her ankle woke her she thought Emmanuel was watching her in the darkness. She hoped she hadn't been groaning with pain in her sleep. Then she was asleep and dreaming Emmanuel was making love to her, slowly and with great sweetness. When she woke with the first call to prayer she thought, I'm leaving Nigeria. She could not stand her loneliness another minute, and she sat up in the near light. She whispered to Emmanuel. "Please come to bed."

They made love. It was as clear and sweet as Diane had dreamed it would be, except that in reality they had to treat her ankle with cautious respect, the way a couple who are not alone must treat creaky bedsprings. Afterwards, Diane kissed Emmanuel and instantly fell into a heavy sleep. When she next awoke, it was light, and Emmanuel was bent in front of the mirror combing his hair.

"We missed your friends," she said. "How will they ever believe I was at your house?"

Emmanuel looked uncomfortable. "Forget all that," he said. "It was a joke." He placed an envelope on her luggage. "I think this will get you to the airport. Please, have a safe journey." And he left the room.

Diane got up to count the money in the envelope. Just then there was a power failure, and the air was suddenly heavy with the smell of sex and sweat and hair tonic. There were three hundred naira in the envelope — more than she had lost.

On her way out a thin child carrying a large vinyl bag was at her heels. The child let her struggle to open the gate with her luggage, and then hissed at her.

"Madam! Your hoto." She held a small black and white ID photograph of Diane — the first picture she had posed for in Nigeria. In it she was wearing no make-up; she'd arrived with the idea that she would feel freer to be her plain self in Africa. Perhaps that was true, but she'd found a kohl pencil for her eyes at the first Sunday market. She smiled now at her smooth, pale mouth and cheeks, her small, bright eyes. In the picture she could have been fourteen years old.

The child was waiting.

Diane asked where she had found the picture.

"On the ground," was the girl's answer.

On the ground in the market?

The girl considered.

"No. Here. Outside the gate. When you were with Emmanuel, Madam."

Then Diane saw it was the prostitute Emmanuel had declared he hadn't slept with — only now she wore rubber thongs and a cheap print wrapper. What had appeared to be enormous, seductive eyes and the high cheekbones of an attractive young woman were no more than the gauntness of a hungry child. In the bag were her working clothes. Diane made out the heel of a shoe.

She had the urge to ask the girl questions. How old are you? Do you feel old? Or do you still feel like a girl? Do you think that what you will do today matters? What about tomorrow? But the girl kept her eyes on the ground and could have been thinking anything at all.

imprimerie gagné ltée

PRINTED IN CANADA